'An original, strikingly confident story' *Independent*

'Brilliant . . . a superbly drawn, complex portrait of adolescence' *Sunday Telegraph*

'Mesmerizing . . . powerful, compelling and memorable' *Guardian*

'A brilliant read' *Herald*

Also by Julie Bertagna

EXODUS
THE OPPOSITE OF CHOCOLATE
THE SPARK GAP

For younger readers

THE ICE-CREAM MACHINE

Julie Bertagna

Soundtrack

YOUNG PICADOR

First published 1999 by Egmont Children's Books Limited

This edition published 2004 by Young Picador
a division of Pan Macmillan Limited
20 New Wharf Road, London N1 9RR
Basingstoke and Oxford
www.panmacmillan.com

Associated companies throughout the world

ISBN 0 330 41813 0

3 5 7 9 8 6 4 2

A CIP catalogue record for this book is available from
the British Library.

Typeset by Intype Libra Limited
Printed and bound in Great Britain by Mackays of Chatham plc, Kent

For my anchors, rescuers and best scavengers ever:
Caroline, Fiona and Graham

Part One

Part Two

Part One

The comet rises from the rim of the ocean until it moves high in the skies over Laggandall Bay. Trails of burnt crystals scatter in its wake. One day, a mote of that celestial litter might fall upon Laggandall's shore, upon this very sand. Right here, where I sit.

Beside the moon, the comet looks fragile. So silent and still. More ghost or angel than a blazing pulse of fire. Though a lone boy on Laggandall Bay must seem small as a speck of cosmic dust to a comet on its glorious voyage across oceans of space.

Here on my patch of Earth, I pulse with life. But every pulsebeat seems to hit a rock wall. I've a comet's rush of energy inside me that has nowhere to go.

I stand and walk to the edge of the black, pounding sea. I shiver, not cold, full of noise. It's around me, inside me, that's all there is. Just an empty shell of a boy and the thunder of the Sound.

I take one last look at the comet's impulse of energy. Then I walk towards the silver gangway the moon has thrown across the waves.

Finn, someone yells.

I walk on.

Salt-stingy hair smears my eyes, seaweed straps round my legs, my jeans are a dragging second skin. Even the waves want to push me back to shore.

But I walk on.

I'm out to my shoulders, out of my depth, caught in the moment, on the track of the call.

A man ploughs towards me through furrows of wave.

Sea-heavy clothes anchor me and I'm caught, flapping and struggling like a netted fish, and brought back in to shore.

Later I lie sleepless and shivering in a cave of bed-clothes. I have to tell myself it was not a dream.

Tonight I almost walked out of the world and into the sea.

Footsteps in my head

This morning is unbelievably blue and still, a perfect day for scavenging. If you were a gull you could fly the whole stretch of the bay without hitting a single puff of cloud. My coorie cove will have scooped in all sorts of brilliant things from the Atlantic, I just know it will. Not that it matters to me because I'll be stuck a zillion miles away in double history with Mr Dow.

Sea tang was on my tongue when I woke this morning and the sound of furious scratching meant Mum was busy herding sand drifts out of the back door. I grabbed a carton of milk and was heading fast for the door when she blocked my escape with her brush.

'I want to talk to you later, Finn!' she yelled as I jumped over the brush to get out the back door, but she looked herself again. She even stuffed a blueberry muffin, my favourite, in my jacket pocket before I escaped. Last night every bit of colour had left her face when Robin's dad dumped me at the door like a sack of sea junk.

'Stupid caper,' the doctor had muttered over me as he listened for water in my lungs.

Dad didn't say a word, the huge energy that's like a fuel box inside him stalled by the shock of what I'd done.

I fell asleep on the shore watching the comet, I told them. I must have been sleepwalking.

But I wasn't.

This morning is much too hot for early March. Face to the sun, I ignore the bare trees on the hills behind and let myself soar in the feeling of summer-blue skies, of days and days of freedom. But this morning I have to sit cooped up in a cramped classroom where the heaters will be on full even though the sun blasts through a wall of windows. And Mr Dow's voice will drone around the room like a dying wasp.

Yet all I'll hear are the words that tramp in my head like a footstep behind each of my thoughts.

Last night I walked into the sea. I was dragged from waves that were as heavy as if they'd fallen from the sky.

I nearly drowned.

The school bus queue is quiet this morning and I wonder if Robin knows about last night and has told the others. I avoid catching his eye because I won't know what to say if he asks me why his dad had to drag me out of the Atlantic. When I steal a glance at Ebbie she makes a silly, sad clown face at me and finishes off the muffin she's decided we're sharing.

'Lentil stew for breakfast,' she announces, and everyone makes sick noises.

It's the only thing that gets any reaction out of the bus queue in the mornings – what Ebbie and the rest of the peace camp have for breakfast. But today I can't laugh.

The noise of the school bus has begun to echo grat-ingly around the bay and the usual lump of dread weighs like a rock in my stomach. More than anything in the world I hate the swish of the bus doors, the sound of the day closing up behind me, wasted, wasted.

The bus follows the line of the bay, just a blue flash in the gaps between houses, sun winking on its windows. I've only moments to act before it's here. I don't care about Mr Dow's stupid double history. More than any-thing I need to be on my own to think about what happened last night. The minute Mr Dow opens his mouth, my head plugs into a compilation of my favourite songs and I learn nothing anyway, so what's the point?

Quickly, I disappear. Ebbie sees me go but she'll never give me away. I've slid down the grass verge to a slab of rock that is out of sight of the road and I wait, watching the waves making lacy frills around the rocks below.

The school bus brakes to a grunty halt. Just along the bay, the windows of my house peep over the rhododen-drons, but they're full of sea light, blind to me.

'Finn?' Ebbie hisses from the edge of the grass verge.

She'll hang about at the end of the queue till the very last moment, hoping I'll reappear before the bus starts, but I won't.

The bus snarls and revs impatiently, then, just as my nerves feel they'll snap, it lets out a loud grumble and gives up on me. The most delicious relief bursts inside as the day opens up like a present. I laugh out loud as every sunbeam in the wide, shimmering bay winks and the footsteps in my head slink away to a corner.

'Where to, then?' I ask a passing gull though I know fine well there's only one place to go on a day like this.

Balancing on a tall rock, I stretch my arms like wings, and bounce gently on puffs of breeze. I jiggle my duffel bag and clank the Coke cans and crisps that I always have with me just in case it's a day I can't face school. Then I check to see what music I've got. My Walkman and music are the pulsebeat that connects me to the outside world. You need that when you live in a nothing-ever-happens, off-the-map place like Laggandall Bay. What I really want is some of my uncle Murray's lazy, wide-open jazz but, rather than settle for something that doesn't quite match the moment, I opt for gull song backed by a running percussion of ocean.

In its secret mooring place under a collapsed rhododendron bush, where my back garden meets the shore, my rowing boat awaits me.

A pagan place

'Um, Finn. About last night. What *was* that?' I ask myself.

It all seems so unreal now that I feel silly bringing the subject up, as if I'm conjuring up a black cloud to spoil this perfect blue day.

I'm waiting until all the fishing boats are in harbour, my launch temporarily abandoned as the bay fills with vessels back from a night catch. I need to keep an eye out too for Grannie Sand. She'd send me packing if she caught me skipping school.

Grannie Sand is guardian angel of the bay. She's also Laggandall's honorary grannie, as good as the real thing to me. When I was tiny I'd tag along with her, learning to scavenge the shore while she told me sea stories of ancient times.

Every morning Grannie clears the sands of litter then explores the sea gifts the ocean has scattered in the night. She gathers flotsam wood to oil and sell as sea heirlooms to summer tourists and watches out for junk I might use. I make things out of sea gifts and my latest creation is the weirdest, the most spectacular junk machine ever.

I'm standing just about at the spot where Robin's dad pulled me out of the sea last night. Waves have smoothed away the drag marks in the sand.

'You nearly drowned yourself, stupid. What's going on?'

No matter how stern I get there's no answer so I start to pull my boat from under its canopy of rhododendron. The harbour is full of the fishing boats that have just swarmed up the Sound, the winding channel of water that leads to the open sea. I decide it's safe to go and row out against the ribs of tide the fleet has made. Baskets of prawns and mackerel clatter on the harbour, distance thinning all sounds till I can't tell human calls from the shouts of fish-scavenging gulls.

I peer at the huddle of fishing boats to check if *The Magnet*, Murray's trawler, is among them but I can't be sure. I look for his blue pullover among the fishermen. Always heavenly blue, for angel luck.

Sunlight makes coloured lanterns of the fizzy drinks the fishermen carry as they leave the harbour. Garnet, emerald and amber: cola, limeade and Irn-Bru. The lanterns switch off as the men vanish round corners and up streets.

I put on my Walkman and turn up the volume as I draw level with the Ministry of Defence naval base – a monstrous, windowless shed. I always have something specially selected, some hi-energy pop or a brash jungle rap to block out that brute of a building. There's only willpower and music to get me past the grey walls and electric fences that are my future if Dad gets his way and I join his business. If I don't, I'll smash his dream of Silverweed and Son, suppliers of killer electric fences to the Ministry of Defence.

Ministry of Destruction, Ebbie calls it. It's the peace camp's nickname. Ebbie's mum, Rachel, helped set up the camp to wage war against the nuclear submarines that prowl the seas around Laggandall. It's eco-war, which means being a non-violent pest to the MoD. I'm not convinced being a pest will rid the planet of the forces of destruction, but Ebbie says time will tell.

'There's that back current,' I remind myself, too late, as I feel the quick tug towards the rocks. I crash sideways on a wave then steady the oars. I nearly drop them a moment later when a fishing boat veers hard round the headland.

The boat noses straight at me, slicing the waves, intent on rushing home. If I don't get out of the way it'll chop through me like I'm a bit of driftwood. But there's no time to do anything.

I recognize the red and blue paintwork of *The Magnet*, close my eyes and stop breathing as the fishing boat heads straight for me. There's an eternity of clattering engine noise and wild, buffeting waves. I'm too terrified to look. Somehow, *The Magnet* misses me and lurches past. I feel the force of it, so close I'm sure I could touch it. Then I'm left crashing about in its wake.

In the wet belly of the boat, I can only hope I might have looked empty and adrift to any crew out on deck. I poke my head above the rim of the boat once the waves calm and the trawler's racket fades to a grumble.

'Murray'll be too busy with the nets and stuff to notice,' a reckless voice whispers, the one that makes me skive school so often.

'He saw you,' Sense reasons. 'He'll tell, and then you've had it.'

'No point in going back then,' Reckless wheedles. 'May as well enjoy the rest of the day.'

I grip the rim of my boat, trembly all of a sudden as I realize what a narrow escape I've had. The trawler missed me by an arm's length.

Across the water, the grey hulk of the naval base looks like a prison. I can't believe that's my future. Days and days of that place, all of my life. I'll never stand it. Yet it's what everyone expects of me. Dad's been telling the whole of Laggandall I'm his future business partner since the day I was born. His love for me is all tied up in the business; every late night and weekend he works is an investment in my future. But his love has become a cage, a cage I can't escape, because to tell Dad I don't want the business, the dream he's worked on for years to pass on to me, would be like telling him I don't love him.

Once upon a time, I thought my whole life was as wide open as the ocean.

There's a groan from the bottom of the boat and I panic as I scrape rock. I steer tight and fast, my arm muscles locking with the strain, till I'm round the head-land and right out of the Sound into the open seas of the Atlantic. The troll rock has its perpetual seagull perched atop. I'm sure it's always the same one. Here now, the Atlantic shelves into rocky shallows. I steer sharply towards shore and at last I feel the drag of soft sand at the base of the boat that tells me I'm snug and safe in the tiny cove that coories deep into the side of the cliffs.

I crash through the water to drag the boat into shore and collapse in the sand, arms floppy and aching from the oars. A can of Coke revives me. Then I put on The Waterboys' 'A Pagan Place', the perfect wild anthem that Ebbie found for the coorie cove, my patch of heaven.

When the track ends my head buzzes with white noise; I had it blasting. It takes a moment to hear the seals that call hello from the tall, shelving cliffs. I stand and wave and at last they fall quiet. The cliffs are odd, tiered like the balconies of a holiday hotel, and pitted with black caves that echo with seal noise. Mermaid Hotel, I call it.

Once, diving for anemones near the balconies, I surfaced beside a rock and found myself nose to nose with a seal and I could see right away why people say they are mermaids in disguise. Those melting eyes could easily lure you to a dark corner of the ocean if you looked a moment too long. Like anemones, a mermaid lures with her beauty. But though the anemone will consume its victim viciously down to shell and bone, its hunger is natural. A mermaid hungers for your very soul.

Out here in my secret cove I can be whatever I want. Some days I'm so happy I scatter like sunflakes on the sea; other times I'm black and wind-shrieked like the cliff caves. The coorie cove doesn't mind. It lets me be.

After a while the seal calls turn urgent but I don't bother right away as I'm too busy scavenging; the best sea gifts always seem to land up here in the coorie cove.

The seals are making a real racket now. I look up and see the waves just beyond the cove churning into foam and I stand on a rock to see what's wrong. As I watch, the foam sucks back into a dark vacuum.

Then the sea explodes.

Noise invasion

A wave-wall surges from the vacuum and a great dark body breaks through. The creature is covered in slimy plankton. It rears up, the sun blurry on its back.

There's a clank-groan and the sea monster's smooth dark body suddenly looks like something more familiar.

A submarine.

I run to the edge of the waves and grab the biggest rock I can handle and fling it but the sub is further out than it looks. Wave after wave churns and chucks sea-weed and litter all over the perfect gold sand of the coorie cove. I'm drenched for the second time in twenty-four hours. I could cry at the mess.

I yell at the sub and pull a string of slimy sea grape off my shoulder. I'm trembling violently. It's colder now the sun is dropping. Not that cold though.

'Finn, stop it,' says my sensible voice. 'It was just a stupid sub.'

Everyone round Laggandall is used to the subs using the Sound as a race track, making crashing reels of tide that upset the whole bay. You don't expect one to come up in your face like that though. And when it reared up like a sea monster I thought this must be my noise terror, the thing that drew me into the waves last night.

And what *did* happen last night? I'm all alone in my coorie cove and I can't escape the questions any more. I sit on a rock and face the thing I don't want to think about – the noises that are haunting me, invading the secret places inside my head.

There's no warning, just all of a sudden my hearing turns so sharp I can hear a crab crawl on the sand. Then my head fuzzes like an untuned radio, full of murmurs and whisperings and dark echoes, as if I'm lost in the whorls of a seashell. The noise builds to a battle clamour, until I feel there's a war raging in my head.

Come away, says a clear, still call at the heart of it all; and I want to. More than anything I want to escape that invasion of noise and go to the clear, still place of the call. And last night I thought I'd found the pathway to it in the silver track of moonlight that led to the depths of the ocean.

Maybe I'm playing too much music. Too much, too loud. Maybe it's some kind of ear problem. But the thought of a life without music is enough to send me walking into the sea. If I didn't have music as a channel to the outside world, I'd crack up. Music is the soundtrack to my life, every bit as much as the ocean.

The day slips past. I check my watch, as I'm sure the coorie cove has different laws of time from the rest of the world. And right enough, it's almost time to pack up. Just another half hour, I promise myself, and begin to scavenge in earnest. The sub has made a real tip of the

place but it just might have churned up something interesting from the seabed.

And it has. Wedged in wet sand at the water's edge is
a top scavenge. A real find.

It's all rusted, full of sand and whelks and seaweed,
but it's a beauty. Black with elegant keys. A real, old-
fashioned typewriter. I put it in the boat and say goodbye to my coorie cove. The seal voices call after me until
I'm past the troll rock and pushing home against the
tide.

Sun-glinted planes swim in the deep blue above me,
tiny silver fish in an endless pond. There's only the
stretch of the Sound to go and I'm home. My house
looks welcoming and cosy among the rhododendrons as
it always does when I've been out adventuring. I burst in
the door as normal around four, and there's Murray
sitting waiting for me at the kitchen table with Mum.

Murray

The three of us look at each other then I settle my gaze on the big blue teapot. Salt lies like grit on my skin and sea-reek is heavy on my school clothes. It feels like a long time before Murray speaks.

'Hard day at school?' he says pleasantly, looking exactly like a Viking without a helmet. His face blazes with ocean-burn and his wild, blond hair is like surfy sea. He looks awkward, odd, because he's wearing a suit with a silky tie and shiny shoes instead of his chunky jumper, jeans and boots. There's a red carnation in his buttonhole.

With a shock I remember the wedding. Anne Marie and Craig – one of Murray's crewmen – are getting married today. Murray is best man and I'm supposed to be minding The Curried Chip for Meera and Ashok so they can see the wedding in the church next door.

Murray takes a gulp of tea and tries to find an angry expression but he looks so unlike himself, with a frown and a suit, that I almost burst out laughing.

'There's nothing funny about coming home in a state like that,' says Mum.

She hesitates and I know she doesn't want to bring up the subject of last night, doesn't know how to, so all she says is, 'You're far too old to be playing round the bay after school. Or in the dark. You've got homework, and things you could be doing for me and your dad, instead of trying to drown yourself. And you stink, you stink of sea!'

She grabs a canister of Forest Breeze air freshener and skooshes clouds of sickly chemical mist around the kitchen. Mum grew up in the city and still feels ocean smells and sand drifts are an invasion of her home.

'Mum!' I swallow the bad taste of air freshener and slip up to my room.

'I want you showered and looking presentable enough for a wedding reception,' she calls as I run for the bathroom.

My blue shirt and best jeans are clean – the ones I've torn and patched and embroidered slogans on for the last two years. They're not exactly weddingy but they *are* a work of art, those jeans.

Murray stops me in my tracks before I reach the front door and hooks me round the neck with his elbow.

'If I ever see you out in the Sound again I'll drag you home in the nets.' He growls the words in my ear so that Mum won't hear. Murray lets go and turns me round to face him. 'I mean it, kiddo. I'll smash that boat of yours to splinters and ground you if I have to. You are not to go out in the Sound. Understand?'

In my whole life I've never seen Murray so serious. He is never totally serious. Even in church you can depend on him to do something like slip a secret cross-eyed look to bring you back from the brink of a boredom-induced coma. It's hard to believe he and Dad are brothers. And yet now that he's all neat and clean-shaven, with that stern look in his eyes, I suddenly see they are alike.

'I can handle the boat, Murray. I've been getting round the Sound all right for years,' I say, whispering though. Mum and Dad would go spare if they knew about the coorie cove. They think I just muck about the shore.

'I know you can handle the sea, Finn, but you can't handle what's under it. Those subs race about the Sound day and night. It's not safe. And neither was today. We nearly crashed you but at least we keep a lookout. I couldn't say the same for some of the joyriders steering the subs.'

Murray is shifting from foot to foot like he's on deck. The boat-timber creak in his voice means he's upset.

'OK, I'm sorry,' I say, the image of that tidal wave of water looming up in my head.

He takes a deep breath. 'Subs aren't big tin fish, Finn. Subs are lethal.'

There's an undercurrent in Murray's voice I haven't heard before. 'You can't predict what they'll do like you can with a tide or even a storm. I've had one rise up in front of me like a whale. And don't tell Lena that. She worries enough.'

Murray looks at me fiercely. In the dim light of the hallway his weather-tan is very dark, his eyes and hair light. I imagine him fighting a crashing sea in a set of Viking horns, instead of a knitted hat that makes his head look like a turnip.

'Course I won't,' I promise.

In the mornings, I often see Lena out walking the bay till Murray's boat is safely home. I'll rap on the school bus windows and make faces down at the twinkies, my pet name for Lena and Murray's toddler twins, who are stuffed in their double buggy with toys and bottles of milk. Lena will be staring out to sea as the twinkies become starfish, all arms and legs, in the excitement of seeing me.

Sometimes she stands beside the Lucky Stone – the great boulder on the harbour that's grooved with ancient wave and fish carvings. It's said that a beached whale stopped the first Norse settlers from starving one long-ago winter when the seas were too vicious to fish. Once the whale had been stripped down to the carcass, there was the Lucky Stone lying in its stomach. The soul of the whale had gone into the stone, Grannie Sand says, and the spirit of the ocean lives in the soul of a whale. No fisherman will set out to sea unless he's touched it.

I give Murray the fisherman's handslap, another Viking leftover, to seal our bargain.

'What's going on out here?' Mum asks suspiciously, but luckily my wedding gear distracts her. 'Is that your idea of presentable?' She groans at my special occasion jeans, gives up and smooths my unruly hair. 'Dandelion head.'

Murray runs me up to The Curried Chip. Craig is waiting for him outside the church, looking panicky.

Murray does the classic forgot-the-ring routine and Craig is so nervous he falls for it. I go into The Curried Chip where Meera and Ashok leave me with a thousand instructions before they run into the church just as Anne Marie's wedding car arrives.

I lean on the counter to get my breath back. In a moment I'll start mixing up batters for the fish and the pakora. Yet right now, I don't know why, but I'm covered in shivers as I look out of the window at the sea glinting like metal, shining like the hard skins of the subs that prowl the floor of the Sound and rise up whenever they choose.

Jingle bells, jellyfish, junk

Outside, the bagpipes are warming up. There isn't a single customer so I bolt the door and run upstairs to see the wedding come out. The muscles in my neck are almost popping as I lean as far out as I can over Ashok and Meera's tiny balcony to get a bird's eye view. Ebbie is among the peace camp people who have brought their hand-made percussion band and are playing a background beat to the naval officer on the bagpipes.

Someone flings a handful of confetti just as Anne Marie and Craig burst out of the church. Anne Marie's veil whips up with the confetti in a twister of wind, and wraps itself like a frothy bandage around Craig's head.

The crowd that's been all around the church begins to ripple like sea anemones as the wedding people spill out on to the street in a foamy rush of pinks and whites and blues that merges with the ordinary colours of the waiting crowd. Little blurs of laughing faces are everywhere.

When Meera and Ashok get back I'm behind the counter, everything disinfected and gleaming and two buckets of batter, spicy and plain, ready in the back shop – though with half the town at the wedding reception it'll be a quiet night.

'Ah!' sighs Ashok, looking as if I've handed him heaven on a plate. 'Off you go and have a nice time.'

When I reach the Laggandall Arms I find Ebbie with Canna and some of the other peace camp people and we all hang around the side door.

Jake, Anne Marie's cousin, slopes over.

'You lot from the peace camp are not invited,' he announces.

Jake's dad is Big Mack, so-called because he owns a small fleet of boats that regularly haul in the biggest mackerel catch on the harbour. Big Mack is big and loud, and has made himself a kind of captain of Laggandall's fishermen, so Jake lives in the wake of his dad's glory and acts like he's really something.

'Not on the official guest list, you're right, but we're hoping for a friendly pass,' says Canna pleasantly in the face of Jake's rudeness and he grins through to Murray at the bar. 'Put in a good word with your uncle, Finn. I could do with a beer.'

'Get in then,' laughs Murray. He's all red and flustered because he's got his speech to do and everyone is pouring in now looking for drinks. 'You lot can be unofficial ushers and help me with the chairs later.'

Ebbie takes off her donkey jacket and suddenly looks quite unlike herself because she's wearing a dress – a long silver-grey, chiffony one with tiny, tinkly metal bells round the hem that match the jingle bells she's taken to braiding through her hair. I've never seen Ebbie in a dress before and I feel shy and strange, just as I did the day I found her years ago fast asleep on the rocks by the naval base – a curled-up little thing, all wet and tatty but kind of beautiful, like a bedraggled mermaid, her hair sandblasted and tangly as seaweed, encrusted with a tiny, sleeping crab. Ebbie is my best scavenge ever.

Robin arrives with his parents and gives me a hard look that sweeps me back to last night and the storm. His dad must have told him about my sea-walking escapade. When he and Jake stand chatting I'm sure it's about me, but when I brush past on the pretext of going to the toilets all I hear is the usual motorbike mania.

'What were you up to last night?' Robin shouts in my ear a bit later though, once the dancing starts. The wedding has erupted for 'Hi Ho Silver Lining' and everyone's yelling the chorus so hard I think the windows will burst. I pretend I can't hear and escape for a drink.

When the song finishes Dad comes over to the bar to argue football with Robin's dad, Murray and Canna from the peace camp. You'd never get this lot talking politics or religion – too dangerous – but football's safe because no matter how heated it gets everybody knows that nobody else's team is much good either.

'What's it to be, Finn?' asks Dad.

Tonight, without his spectacles and business frown, he looks years younger; and now he's standing beside Murray I'm struck by their resemblance for the second time today. It's as if each of them has, for the evening, swapped places. Murray, tamed and unusually tense in the role of best man, could almost be Dad in his business suit. While Dad, unusually relaxed, his face flushed and hair messed from dancing, has a look of Murray

21

fresh in from the sea. All the boxed-up energy he usually packs into his work has been let loose on the dance floor. Embarrassingly loose. Parents shouldn't be allowed to dance in public.

'Beer?' I try. 'Small beer?'

'Try again,' laughs Dad. 'Try a Coke. In fact, try sticking to Cokes from now on.'

Robin's dad winks at me and I see they've all decided beer was at the root of my antics last night.

Dad hands over three Cokes. 'Tell Ebbie and Robin to keep you out of trouble.'

When I get back Ebbie and Robin are on the dance floor, doing a silly clodhopping barn dance, Ebbie's braided hair whipping all over her face.

Robin leans over to make his feet step in time to Ebbie's and looks into her face every moment or two. They stomp faster and faster until they're completely out of time with the music. As I watch them, so happy and close, I feel an unpleasant lurch inside as if I got caught in a freak wave out on my boat.

Ebbie tosses the braids from her face as they clodhop past. We make eye contact for a second.

'What happened last night?' Ebbie asks later, when the slow dances calm the place down. Her voice vibrates against the music, close to my ear, and makes icy trails on my neck. 'Robin told me his dad dragged you out of the sea in the pitch dark. And then you skip school again. What's going on?'

'Stupid caper,' I say, echoing the doctor because I don't know what to say.

'Uhuh,' she says. 'I was wondering, after you were

talking the other day about some kind of odd noise you were hearing, if it was anything to do with that?'

She's too sharp, Ebbie. You tell her something or she reads a detail in a book, things anybody else would forget right away, and it all gets logged away in that computer brain of hers. She's determined to be the most clued-up eco-warrior on the planet.

Mum is shepherding Dad and Murray away from the bar in the direction of the door while Lena tries to catch the twinkies who are still zapping around the hall like little firecrackers. They'll be all burned out tomorrow.

'Come with us,' I urge Ebbie, and she gets her jacket. The tiny bells on her dress and in her hair make a kind of fairy music and I tune into it as we separate from the others on the walk home round the bay. The music from the Laggandall Arms blurs once we're down on the shore, but there are echoes of it on the waves as if the wedding is out at sea. The sky and the bay are full of lights. The comet is right above us.

'I think it's a ghost or an angel,' I tell Ebbie. 'Not a comet, after all. Comets are supposed to blaze across the skies.'

'Angel's breath. That's what it looks like,' says Ebbie. 'Although it's really just the combustion of frozen gases.'

'Don't spoil it, Ebbie. It's a bit of magic and I don't want you explaining it away. Do you know we'd have to live another four thousand years before we see that comet again? In all the times and places it could be it's come now, here in our lives. Amazing.'

'I do know,' says Ebbie drily. 'Because I told you. Do you know what all the talk is though?' She leans near

23

and I'm enclosed in a flurry of fairy music that sends shivery trails all over me. 'Everyone's saying a comet is a bad omen, a harbinger of doom, and as long as it hangs over us we're all in the grip of the forces of darkness. A bunch of women were in a real tizzy about it in the toilets,' she laughs and nods back towards the Laggandall Arms. 'Your aunt Lena was one of them.'

'Lena gets a bit demented when Murray's due out at sea. He's away for a long haul next week, a two-week mackerel chase. That comet's the last straw.'

All of a sudden I'm trembly as I watch the comet, hanging there like a ghost or an angel of doom. What if my noises are some dark force brought in its wake? But I'm being stupid. Ebbie can explain the comet easily enough with one of her science lectures, and there's bound to be a rational explanation for the noises. They could just be submarine echoes in the bay.

'Of course Lena's worried. Stupid me.' Ebbie sounds guilty.

I was sharp just then and she'll think I'm annoyed that she laughed at Lena.

'But she gets pretty silly too.' I jingle one of the hair bells and smile. 'Sews bits of rowan twig dipped in Holy Water into Murray's jumpers. Says prayers as she ties wind knots and puts on all her pot lids when it's stormy to keep the weather in check. You can't tell Lena superstition and religion don't mix – she'll try anything if she thinks it'll keep Murray safe at sea.'

'Poor Lena,' says Ebbie.

'Yeah,' I say, feeling bad because Lena's all right, really. Just a nervous wreck.

'Look,' says Ebbie. She leans forward and points at a patch of sea glitter. 'What is *that*?'

I look. The rocks and stones all along the shore are glossed with soft moonlight. But they seem to merge and separate, neither rock nor liquid, something molten in between the two states.

'Yuk,' says Ebbie.

'What's happened?' I breathe.

I step off my rock and poke a foot at the gleaming sliminess, then jump back but it doesn't move, just lies in a great mass of raggedy patches. Ectoplasm, I suddenly think, the stuff of ghosts. I draw back, wondering about things that have died in the sea – then I see what it is.

'Jellyfish! Look, they're all over the water. Hundreds of them.' I crouch and with a stick I carefully lift one, flopping it over. 'I think they're dead.' I stare up at Ebbie. 'They swam out of the oceans and up the whole of the Sound to reach us here and then they died. Lena would say it means something.' I try to laugh but can't.

Reflections of the red light alarm system on the naval base run like trails of blood across the black waters of the bay. Ebbie stares hard. 'More likely to be some kind of pollution from that lethal blot on the landscape. Unlucky jellyfish.'

Ebbie's face is dappled by sea light. With her wispy dress and her jingle bells she could be an Arabian princess – the clumpy, silver-painted Doc Martens kind of spoil the effect.

'Cocteau Twins' "Essence"!' she suddenly announces. And she's right. Turned up loud it would be the perfect soundtrack for this huge blackness of sea and sky scattered with moon and stars and comet, red lights and glistening jellyfish. And it's the sound of Ebbie too, somehow; the feeling of being here with her tonight.

She catches me watching her, comes over and stares back at me with eyes like moonlit rockpools. 'Now, tell me about last night.'

'I'm wiped out, Ebbie. I'm off home now,' I say, shivering. For some reason I can't look her in the eyes any more. I long to stay with her yet it's something in the very force of this ache that unnerves me and makes me go.

I walk along the sand to the shore steps that lead to my back garden, listening to Ebbie's jingle bells until the sound is swallowed up by wind-billows and the fold of the sea. What's bothering you? I ask myself. Everything, is the answer. There are my noises, the fact that I nearly drowned myself last night, a sea full of dead jellyfish, and the comet that hangs over us like angel's breath or a harbinger of doom.

And something about Ebbie unsettles me too. Maybe it's just that tonight she seemed like a fairy princess with her jingle bells and wispy dress among all the glitter of the bay. Yet it's not only tonight I've felt as if I'm haunted by her, as if some invisible part of her lingers with me once she's gone. I've felt that for a long time. But tonight some secret energy of hers has touched me, some magnetic, magical force that I never knew she had has caught me up and tugs at my heart with the pull of the tide.

*

'Help me with the washing, Finn?' yawns Mum from the back lawn. 'These sheets will be as stiff as salt cod if I leave them out till the morning. It's turning cold.'

'Nice girl, Ebbie,' says Mum, as we fold the crackly sheets. 'Your dad likes her too. Says she's clever.'

'Too nice and clever to be a peace camp troublemaker, you mean.'

'Now, Finn,' says Mum, her voice low and soft. 'And while we're out here you can explain about last night.'

I sigh. How can I tell her about my noises without sounding as if I've gone mad? She'll jump to all the wrong conclusions – drink, drugs, loud music, late nights. I should have been born a seagull. If I was a seagull I could fly the world. Seagulls don't have problems with their parents. They don't have to explain themselves to anyone. You don't put seagulls in classrooms or map out futures for them.

Mum sighs back at me as I stay silent. But she knows when to let me be, so she just reaches up and ruffles up my hair a bit and goes inside. I carry in the washing basket then slip back out to the storm-battered boatshed on the shore at the bottom of the garden. I light my paraffin lamp, put some shimmery, sizzling techno storm in my Walkman and turn up the volume as I sit back to survey my junk machine.

She's quite something.

The last one you had to wind up by hand but this one's fully mechanized. I remember the typewriter scavenged from the coorie cove, still in the boat, but as I turn to get it I'm confronted by Murray standing in the doorway, his face creased up and tears streaming down his cheeks.

I snap off the music. 'What's happened?'

Murray whimpers and I grab him in a panic. He gives one of his boat-timber creaks and I realize he's in fits over my junk machine, in an agony of laughter, helpless with it. He's also had one too many beers.

'Time you were in your bed,' I tell him. I can't help laughing at him laughing. And the junk machine *is* a ridiculous sight.

Murray rattles through my scatter of disks on the floor, shakes his head at my musical taste then grabs one as if he's found gold. It'll be REM. His favourite track is 'Texarkana' because he says he's the guy who's had 20,000 wasted chances yet he's still got 40,000 reasons to live.

'Take it,' I tell him.

'Take all your chances, Finn,' he tells me as he always does. He staggers a bit.

'Time you were in bed,' I tell him again. 'Lena will be worrying.'

'Just needed some air after being cooped up indoors half the day.' Murray pats the junk machine's birdcage body and the movement jerks her long, moony face towards him. 'I've never seen anything like it,' he splutters. 'Finn, my boy, you'll go far!'

As he staggers off into the night, that crackshot laugh of his bouncing off the rocks and ringing through the dark, I remember the jellyfish graveyard, but he's too tipsy to notice tonight. I'll ask him about it tomorrow. Murray's as superstitious as any fisherman. He'll know what a sea full of dead jellyfish means.

Reckless again

All night, Atlantic rollers crash through my dreams of dead jellyfish, the vibrations sending shivers through the netted sea creatures caught above my bed. I wake up fuzzy-headed from a bad night's sleep.

My bedroom is a sea forest with walls of silver-streaked midnight blue that are like the sea under moonlight. The canopy is a bit of old fishing net from Murray's boat, filled with sea urchins and starfish from the coorie cove's rockpools.

Wind bangs doors and the house shudders. Pulling on any old clothes because it's Saturday, I run downstairs trying out the tastes of bacon roll, fried egg roll and toasted cheese in my head, and decide to have one of everything.

'Hungry, are we?' grins Mum. 'I'm not surprised, it's past lunchtime.' She's sweeping up the sand the wind tucks into every corner and crevice during the night.

'Your dad's got some Saturday work for you up at the base.' She looks at me uneasily.

'I've already got a Saturday job at The Curried Chip,' I remind her. 'I'm there this afternoon.'

Mum stops sweeping and puts a dispirin tablet in a glass of water. I watch it fizzle and dissolve into sandy sediment at the bottom of the glass.

'Sore head?' I grin.

'Don't do as I do . . .' she laughs. 'Now listen, Finn. It's no use turning down everything your dad can give you if you've not even tried it.'

'I have tried it. I spent all last summer picking fried rabbits and seagulls off Dad's killer fences, remember?'

Mum wrinkles up her nose. 'It's not all like that. Why don't you talk to him and find something you enjoy? There are lots of things you could learn. The business forecast – that's exciting.' She nods at a spread of paper on the table. 'Or you could get to grips with the computer side of things.'

I groan. None of it interests me. And lately, whenever Dad and I talk it's been like walking on eggshells, tiptoeing around each other to avoid the subject that stands between us, as charged and dangerous as an electric fence. My future.

'What litter that weather will have thrown up all over the rhododendrons again,' Mum breaks off, seeing it's no use.

I block out the pictures of a sea like forked-up jelly that filled my dreams last night.

'Go on up to the base,' says Mum, and shoves some money into my hand as a peace token, or a bribe.

I walk up the hill to the MoD naval base, turn my back on the clinical grey waste of it and step through the bramble bush archway into the gaudy clutter of painted caravans, washing lines and vegetable plots that is the peace camp.

Here among the cramped caravans there's a pulse of ragged energy that's a world away from Laggandall's neat curve of pastel-pretty cottages.

Ebbie's six-year-old brother Felix waves from the grass, his mouth wide and waiting for Ebbie to feed him another mouthful of spaghetti. A mechanical dance beat is thumping from their caravan.

I sit down beside them and look to see what Ebbie's reading today. Kafka.

'It's about a man who wakes up one day and he's an insect,' says Felix enthusiastically. 'Ebbie's reading it to me. I love it.'

'You would.' I grin at Ebbie. 'Does Kafka go with trashy pop?' It's not really what you'd expect an intellectual young eco-warrior to be listening to.

'Not my choice,' says Ebbie, brittle because she's embarrassed. 'I wanted Dvorak.'

Felix and I swap grimaces.

'Trashy pop's better for eating spaghetti to,' says Felix. 'Look, I can slurp in time to the beat.'

'Felix! I'm splattered.'

Ebbie hands me Felix's bowl and goes into her caravan. With its herb and vegetable patch, bricked-in barbecue and tree swing it's about as mobile as my house. But it's painted red all over with great yellow flowers, as if a four-year-old giant has been let loose on its walls with a paintbox. Next door is a bumblebee.

I feed Felix, leaning back to avoid the slurpy splash as he reaches the end of each string of spaghetti.

'D'you want to see my insect jars again?' Felix asks. He has an insect prison under the caravan: jars and jars of insects trying to struggle out to each other through the glass of their prison walls. It doesn't exactly fit with the peace camp's Protect the Planet ethos.

'They're nasty and cruel, Felix,' I tell him.

'Please go and play with a nuclear sub,' Ebbie sighs. She's changed her splattered top to a rainbow-knit.

We walk down to the shore and it's so quiet I wonder if you could wipe Laggandall off the face of the earth and no one would notice. Along at the naval base Dad is waiting for me to help unpluck the daily fry-up of rabbits and seagulls off the electric fences, but there's no sign of him.

We skid down the grass slope to the rock slabs and I steal glances at Ebbie but she looks just like herself again and I've got none of the strange shivers of last night.

'I've been feeling a bit weird, Ebbie,' I blurt out.

She looks at me quickly. Of course she knows. People don't go sea-walking for nothing. But she's known for a while, I'm sure.

We jump through a gap in the rocks to the patch of sandy beach that is invisible from the road.

'Tell me,' she urges.

'I'm due in The Curried Chip soon. I can't just spill it out. It's complicated. Kind of stupid.'

'Then I'll see you tomorrow, after your Sunday morning stint at The Curried Chip. I'll pop in for my usual then we can go to your cove. I'm babysitting Felix tonight.'

Ebbie's usual, which I invented for her, has turned into The Curried Chip special that everyone wants: pakora and chips, smothered with curry sauce, in a bread roll. Ashok thinks it's horrible but he says I'm a genius for inventing such a profitable food craze.

'Finn!'

It's Dad. I drop down behind a rock, knowing he's seen me, but Reckless tells me to ignore his angry shouts from behind the electric fence, to grab Ebbie's hand and run until I can't hear him any more.

Now I'm for it. But as Ebbie and I race each other all the way round the bay, Reckless just laughs in the face of the wind and says worry about it later.

Talk of the town

Sunday mornings my bedroom stinks of curry and chips. It's in my hair, on my skin, everything. I finish at The Curried Chip around midnight on Saturdays and have to be hauled out of bed for church next morning, too late to shower, so I sit there smelling like a day-old fish supper with a side portion of curry sauce.

Ashok always starts to fry up when he hears the final hymn. The Curried Chip is right next door, stuck bang in the middle of the town's two churches. The smell of chips creeps along the pews and activates a chorus of tummy-rumbling that even reaches Father Marion. His rumbles get broadcast over the pulpit microphone, which sets the whole congregation sniggering and gets him so upset he's like an angry sergeant-major hollering the final blessing at us.

I race out before the bedlam of two congregations hits The Curried Chip.

'Ah, Finn,' says Ashok gratefully, in his half-Indian, half-Scottish accent. Ashok speaks like he's reciting a poem, in a trip-trip rhythm. 'And a nice smile, please, for my Sunday customers, come on.'

Meera rescues me before Ashok gives me a hundred instructions. Meera is a gem.

'Leave him alone,' she tells Ashok and flings the fish-shimmery tail of her blue sari over her shoulder. There's something about the way she does it that turns Ashok sheepish. He goes into the back shop.

He'll be back out like a shot when he sees the queue that's just gathered. A queue always panics him, yet it's the very thing he wants.

I can't sneak Ebbie too many extra chips as Ashok is right at my elbow but I tell her to meet me at the boat-shed afterwards. I'm finally going to introduce her to my junk machine. It's been top secret till now.

'Come on, come on, come on,' panics Ashok. 'The queue, the queue, the queue. Never mind the girlfriend chatting.'

I blush till my ears burn and Ebbie scoots off.

I shovel chips into cartons and splash curry sauce over them. I flip fish and hamburgers and pakora out of the hotplate with blistering fingers, fling ladlefuls of rice and Ashok's special curry into foil cartons.

And then, out of nowhere, it comes.

Someone turns up the volume inside my head and the creaky ice-cream sign outside the door begins to make an unbearable racket. It's like a saw, slicing through the noise of the queue, through my head. A crowd of guys from the naval base are all talking and laughing at once, yet the ice-cream sign is almost drowning them out.

'Thanks, next please, yes?' I chant, glancing out the window. Ebbie is sitting on Robin's moped and as she smiles up at him I have that unpleasant lurching inside,

35

a sensation that, for a second, cuts through everything else.

'Single fish, no vinegar and just a little salt, Finn. Feeling better today?'

I'm face to face with my history teacher, Mr Dow. I grab a bit of fish and sprinkle too much salt.

'Just a tummy bug, Mr Dow. There you go.'

I smile brightly but Mr Dow isn't going yet.

'Ah, yes. Prone to those, aren't you? And you'll be back at school tomorrow?'

He just stands there and looks at me and fiddles at the place where his tie would be if he wasn't wearing a polo neck. I'm willing him to go because the noise, the one that I dread, is here now – just a tiny thing like an itch or a wasp at the back of my head – but it's there, whispering, murmuring.

'Come on, come on, come on,' chants Ashok, hovering beside Meera, who is calm as a statue over by the till.

The guys from the naval base have quietened to an impatient shuffle; they look as if they could give Mr Dow a shove along. I wish they would.

'Tomorrow lunchtime. You come and see me.' Mr Dow nods at Ashok and Meera and leaves at last. My stomach feels draggy like it does before an exam.

If panic had a noise, Ashok would be fizzling like a blob of sherbet in water. Mr Dow has just lost him the naval guys who got fed up waiting and opted for lunch at the pub.

I serve everyone at top speed, not even bothering that I'm flinging chips and splattering sauce everywhere

36

because the whisperings and murmurings are echoing all through my head.

And then it happens and there's nothing I can do.

A terrible, crashing wave of noise breaks and I'm sucked into it. I start to disintegrate, caught up in a force so overwhelming it will pull me out of the world. And in that moment, on the edge of a void, I move. I run out of the shop.

I have no thoughts or feelings at all as I smash the creaking Wall's ice-cream sign through the window of The Curried Chip.

'Psycho,' says a voice I don't know. One of the fishermen or a naval officer. I'm on the ground, feeling blurry.

'His mum and dad are coming,' says Meera. 'I phoned.' She's talking over my head at Ebbie. 'He's drunk? On a Sunday morning?'

Meera stares down at me, horrorstruck. I realize a lot of people are staring. Now the whole town knows there is something wrong with me.

'Hey,' says Ebbie, trying to sound as if it's not the end of the world but there's a breathiness in her voice. She's as shocked as everyone else. I can't look at her for a while but when I do I see there's a splatter of blood on her face. I stare at it, sickened.

'Oh, it's just . . .' She wipes it away with her hand, looks at her fingers and shrugs.

I can't believe what I've done.

'I'll meet you at the boatshed in the morning,' murmurs Ebbie, as my parents arrive in the car. 'We'll skip school and go out to the cove, OK?'

I can't believe she's really said that. Ebbie never skips school. But more than that, she wants to see me, even though everyone else is staring at me like I'm crazy. Or psycho. She even smiles – a brave, brittle wee smile – as the car draws away and I hold on to her words like an anchor to get me through whatever I have to face with Mum and Dad.

Dad usually keeps himself thoroughly in check. Yet even when he's doing the most ordinary things, reading the paper or watching football on TV, you can feel the huge energy drive that's built up a thriving one-man business from nothing. It's like an Atlantic gale kept in a box. Now it has all turned to rage and disappointment and he's struggling to control it, turning on Mum, demanding that she explain my behaviour, as if he can hardly bear to look at me and remind himself that the talk of the town really is his own son.

'I don't understand it,' he says at last.

Neither do I, so what can I say? Silently, I slip out of the living-room and out the back door. Alone in the boatshed I fling on my Walkman and make the music loud.

Dad might not even notice I'm gone. When he looks at me these days it's not really me he's seeing, not me as I really am; it's as if he once slipped a glowing ghost-image of the son he imagines me to be over the real me, and he's come to believe in it. And I've found myself living in its shadow, pretending that I am the ghost-boy, living up to his wonderful illusion.

Except now the real me has torn free of the shadow,

and Dad is left looking in bewilderment at the two of us
– at the empty skin of the ghost-boy and at this flesh-
and-blood oddity, an embarrassment that has jumped
out, like a freakish Jack-in-the-box, from the son he
thought I was. And he can't bear the shattering of the
illusion any more than I can.

Doom eager

The rest of that day the house is so silent you'd think somebody had switched off the volume. I escape to the boatshed and pump my head full of songs that seem to know all about me. The whole world fades as I flood myself with sound. Now it's just me and the music. When I emerge on to the shore I feel as if my head has exploded then put itself back together again.

'So there you are. What do you think this is, Finn?'

Grannie Sand holds up a long bit of metal. She doesn't mention that she hasn't seen me for a fortnight even though we live next door to each other. I come to see her when I want to and she likes that. Right now I need her.

'Looks like a metal hockey stick,' I say. 'What is it?'

'A metal hockey stick?' she chuckles, her eyes sparkling like two bits of sea and just as changeable. 'A wicked one that would be on somebody's shins. I'll put it in the Haven't A Clue pile until one of us has a brainwave.'

'Grannie,' I say, wondering how to begin.

'You're in trouble, I hear,' she says, helpfully.

I take a breath. 'Something weird is going on in me. Something I don't understand.'

Grannie Sand wipes the metal hockey stick thing with a wet cloth. We sort out the pile of scavenges into junk and litter, and in between examining the bits and bobs I tell her about my noises.

Grannie stoops over a bit of unidentifiable plastic.

'Doom eager. Now I wonder if that's what it is.'

She champs her teeth after she says the curious phrase, as if she's chewing on it.

I look at the plastic thing, wondering what a doom eager is until I realize she means me.

'Doesn't sound too healthy,' I say, as Grannie wipes hands so mucky they look like they've been dredging an oil slick. 'Anyway, it's either my hearing or I'm sick in the head. Is that what doom eager means?' I don't really want to think about either option. Just now, my ears seem fine and I don't feel mad.

Grannie Sand scrunches up her sea-sparkle eyes and explains: 'It's in the blood, I'm sure, from centuries of living beside the might of the sea. You're open to all sorts of currents and forces because you're so much a part of it. Something catches you up and turns you doom eager. You know, Finn, I'm sure the ancient ways still haunt us. There's Old Norse in our souls. Those Vikings knew all about doom eager; it's what took them out to sea. Here in Laggandall Bay, one way or another, we're all in the thrall of something. What's caught you?' Grannie Sand squeezes my shoulder before wandering off along the shore, bent like a tree that's been in the Atlantic winds too long.

I wander in the opposite direction, thinking about doom eager. The usual gang sits on the harbour wall, Robin among them. Jake too, which is bad news. Still, I venture over, but Jake turns and stares at me in a way that tells me he saw my spectacle at The Curried Chip.

He looks at me as if I'm a sea slug he'd like to jump on and squish.

I've never liked Jake. He always seems to reek of pickled onion crisps and there's a sneer at the edge of everything he says. Picking on people is his favourite pastime. But in a place the size of Laggandall your choice of mates is limited and Jake's redeeming quality is a CD collection that runs the length of a bedroom wall. He also has an electric guitar, which he can't play, but that doesn't stop him. He sits out with the harbour gang in the dark, trying to be a guitar hero with his tiny amplifier. Murray says he puts the fish in shock.

'Loony tune,' he mutters, and advances.

I want out of here. Now.

Robin steps in front of Jake to give me time. I take my chance and run.

Once I get my breath back and the blood in my head stops thumping, I realize I'm in the last place on earth I want to be. Just across the road, back in its usual place, creaks the ice-cream sign. The Curried Chip's window is boarded-up and there's a neat pile of glass beside the door. Before I can make my feet move Meera comes out with a brush and shovel.

She sees me and a frown tightens her delicate features. I know she's more shocked than angry and I want to tell her I'm sorry but at that moment Ashok appears. The ferocious look on his face tells me it's time to run again and I don't stop until I'm safe in the boatshed with my junk machine. I put on some head-bursting thrash metal, the loudest music I own, and turn it up as high as I can stand it.

I flop down on the floor and let the music wipe me out.

Then I nearly jump out of my skin because Murray is staring at me through the bars of the junk machine's bird-cage body. He comes over beside me. I switch off the Walkman and we sit there in the gloom of the boatshed, nice and quiet, for a while.

'Drugs? Drink?' Murray says gently. I listen closely but there's no anger in his voice, not even disappointment. Just concern. Relief is warm. 'Not your style though, eh, Finn?'

'I'm sorry.' It's all I can say.

Murray is just a fisherman but he knows the patterns of clouds and stars, tides and weather. The other fishermen call him the Herring King because he has such a feel for the spirit of the sea that he can track the elusive herring shoals to their secret places in the great halls of the ocean. He knows when something is out of its normal pattern. Gone agley, he would say. Murray understands that I've gone agley.

'Don't worry, kiddo,' he smiles at me. 'I don't know what's up, and I don't know if you do either, but I'm fighting in your corner. Always remember that.'

All night long words swim in my head. Doom eager. Loony tune. Psycho. They drum to the beat of the Atlantic outside. But through it all is Murray; a clear, still voice telling me he's fighting in my corner against whatever it is that's caught me up and holds me in its grip.

A careless drowning

'Draw a cat,' says Ebbie.

'A cat?'

She's here at the boatshed as she said she would be, skipping a whole Monday of school, just for me. I don't even care that she's brought along a thumping great medical encyclopaedia. After telling her the other day that I couldn't just blurt out what was wrong, I ended up blurting everything out the minute I saw her this morning.

'If the cat looks like it's shimmering—'

'*Shimmering?*'

'If it looks as if the drawing is breaking up, as if the edges, the outer molecules of the cat are crumbling, then it indicates the inner self is too. Aural hallucination – that's hearing things – is a serious form of psychosis, a kind of unconscious invasion.'

Just in case I wasn't already worried.

'What exactly is psychosis?' I ask.

Psycho. Someone called me that yesterday outside The Curried Chip.

There's a pause as Ebbie finds the place in the book.

'It's when an individual's contact with reality becomes distorted. Often there's a special strategy a person invents to live in an unliveable situation. Sounds like you, doesn't it?'

It does.

'So a special strategy might be silly noises? This is all to do with me not wanting to join my dad's business?' Ebbie knows well enough how I feel about that. She's been telling me for ages that I must speak to Dad but she doesn't understand that you can live in the same house as someone all your life and never really speak to them.

'I didn't invent those noises, Ebbie,' I tell her. 'I hate them. Why would I invent something I hate?'

'Just draw a cat.' Her tone softens. 'Don't worry. Once we know what it is we can get you the right sort of help.'

'Don't talk to me like a doctor. Would you like it if you thought you might be mad? And now you've told me about the cat, I'll only draw unshimmery, unpsy-chotic ones, won't I?'

'Oh,' says Ebbie. Her rockpool eyes look at me, troubled and full because she thinks she's let me down.

I sit on a rock and do her a cat that's the very oppo-site of what I feel. A solid, happy cat with thick felt pen edges and a got-the-cream cartoon face.

The sky is solid and waves are spitting froth all over the side of the boat when we push out. A luminous salt-mist hangs in the air, smudging everything so that it looks out of focus.

Murray's submarine warning is shoved to the back of my head because I'd risk anything to escape to my coorie cove with Ebbie for the day. *The Magnet* is far out on the

Atlantic on its marathon mackerel chase, so there's no chance of any more close encounters with Murray.

'So I'm risking death for you, Finn Silverweed,' says Ebbie when I tell her about my near-miss with *The Magnet* and the sub explosion the other day. 'I know *all* about the subs. It's my mum's obsession, remember. Mum says the subs are big alley rats scuttling among all the junk and bones on the seabed. Anyway, you can always spot a sub. There's a certain look about the surface of the ocean. A particular kind of ripple.'

'You're on sub duty, then,' I tell her as I steer us out of rats' alley and into the Atlantic.

The coorie cove feels all in a fret today. That brute of a submarine upset it the other day. But I'm happy and free, from everything that bothers me.

Ebbie has brought along her CD player and puts on The Waterboys' 'This Is The Sea', an eco-spiritual sound-scape full of wind and ocean. It's a peace camp favourite. The first track begins with an almighty clamour that could rouse the gods. It crashes off the cliffs, making a great amphitheatre of the cove.

'Amazing,' says Ebbie, when it ends. She's right beside me, making finger patterns in the sand. The wind tugs at her long hair that's like the seaweed tangles on the rocks, so there's a constant murmur of fairy bells in the air. Once again, I feel that strange shiver as if she's not really Ebbie but some magical girl, with a kind of glimmer about her like the soft moon gleam on the shore pebbles at night.

'Do you know what else would be amazing? A house, built right into the cliffs,' she is telling me.

Ebbie points up to the cliff balconies that an eternity of wind and waves have hollowed out. The seals lie sluggishly on them like stubborn sunbathers even though there's not a speck of sun in the sky.

'A house where there's only the sea and the sky,' Ebbie continues. 'Finn, let's climb up and see. Let's go cave exploring.'

There's a silent space that the wind and the waves fill.

'What's up?' says Ebbie. 'Have you never explored them? It looks like you could climb up easily enough—'

'No!'

Ebbie stares at me. I'm trembling. I can see the thought in her eyes as clearly as if she'd spoken it out loud. I hear those voices from yesterday outside The Curried Chip: psycho, loony tune.

'I don't like caves.'

'Don't like caves?' Ebbie screws up her face. 'Don't like *caves*?'

I decide a light touch is my best way out.

'Nasty, dark places full of sea slugs and mermaids that could mesmerize a boy and lure him to the depths of the sea. For all eternity.'

Those black, echoing mouths are the only thing that spoil the coorie cove. The wind booms through them into the labyrinth of tunnels that run deep into the cliffs and the noise haunts the cove. Once, ages ago, I climbed up the balconies and ventured inside one. It was like standing inside a seashell with swirling echoes of wind and sea all around. Things slithered deep inside the caves and though I told myself it was just the seals, I was terrified. I couldn't get back down to the shore quick enough. A million pounds wouldn't get me inside those caves again.

'But I'm a girl so I'd be all right,' smiles Ebbie.

'There might be mermen. In fact, a hermit once lived in those caves, long ago. Grannie Sand said he spied a mermaid out at sea and followed her here in his boat. He was so entranced by her he spent the rest of his days in the caves watching for her. He might still be there.'

Still doom eager for his mermaid.

'Poor hermit,' says Ebbie. She wrinkles up her face. 'He'll be a pile of bones if he's still up there. I won't bother. Hey, what's that?' She breaks off and runs over to the rocks. I watch her footprints smooth out and disappear in the damp and spongy sand.

From where I sit, I can only see Ebbie's top half. Her shoulders heave and strain as if she's dragging a dead weight. I go over and see it's a bit of old fishing net she's trying to haul. Something lumpen and slimy lies in the netting, like the flesh of a monstrous mussel shell. Its eye locks with mine. A fixed gaze.

It's a seal.

'I think it's dead,' Ebbie gasps. 'Help me. It must've drowned in the netting.'

'Dead!'

'Get a grip, Finn,' breathes Ebbie.

She doesn't understand. Though he harvests the sea, Murray says a fisherman must respect its laws and creatures. Not to do so is to risk the wrath of the oceans. A seal carelessly drowned in a fisherman's net is bad enough. But if that seal is really a mermaid, it means tragedy and we'll pay for it.

We untangle the seal from the herring net and try, awkwardly, to bring it back to life. Ebbie massages where she thinks a seal's heart should be while I splash Coke on its lips. I get the rug from the boat and tuck it around the solid body, then clear the strands of maiden's hair seaweed that have caught around the mouth. We roll the seal on its side and try pumping water out of it the way Robin's dad did when he pulled me out of the sea. But the seal sounds dull and solid inside and its oily brown eyes are fixed on the sky. I turn and follow its gaze. There's a giant's fist of rain-cloud breaking the solid grey, nothing else. Nothing but a waspy noise, as annoying as an itch, at the back of the coorie cove.

Ebbie suggests we return the seal to the sea where it belongs so we grip the fishing net and haul the seal over the rocks till we can empty it into the sea.

It goes in with a clunking sound, like an old ship's bell hitting the floor of the sea. Except the seal never hits the bottom; the murky bronze body seems to inflate like a balloon and floats back up till it is bobbing around the surface. All the time the wasping noise grows louder and louder until it's a ferocious clattering. And the seal's dead eyes stare at a point in the sky as if they can see some horror that's invisible to us, erupting in the blank grey.

War at sea?

When the first one comes it bursts out so sudden and jerky I think it has jumped off the cliff. I grab Ebbie and put my hands up to shield our heads as I wait for the thing to fall on the sand.

There is another, and another. The furious clattering rebounds off the cliffs in waves of echoes.

Helicopters. They hurtle like rocks above our heads. In seconds the sky is chuck-full of them.

'A naval exercise,' mutters Ebbie. 'That's all.'

We kick at the sand, laugh a bit, embarrassed at the shock they've given us.

Then the waves come – booming, crashing Atlantic rollers full of the wrath of the ocean. There is no storm and no tide due in. Seaspray soaks us because we're rooted to the spot, watching the ocean now. The helicopters so surprised us we hadn't seen the shoal of things that have all of a sudden cluttered the waters beyond the cove – a sub, a massive minesweeper, the town's two lifeboats and a fleet of fishing trawlers.

It looks like war at sea.

'What's happening?' cries Ebbie.

She grabs my hand but I can't answer because I feel I'm drowning in noise: the noise of all those vessels junking up the sky and sea, filling the coorie cove with swarms of echoes. I clamp my hands to my ears to block it out. But I can't block the other noise, my noise, the one that has started like an itch at the back of my head and is growing, stretching itself right to the very brim, the very edges of me, until I feel I'm going to split and splinter into a million bits right here on the sand.

Come away, says a strong, still call.

I stagger towards the sea. Ebbie catches me, her eyes like torn bits of sky.

'It's all right, Finn,' she says, after a while. 'They're all gone.'

Ebbie holds me safe for what feels like a very long time, until all the shattered bits of me bind together again, only to begin to disintegrate once more. But this time it's the sweetest, softest of meltings, a relief that lets me dissolve in the gentle strength of her arms, a feeling I don't want ever to end.

I lie in the belly of the boat all the way home. I'm always exhausted after a noise attack. Ebbie rows us, managing the currents at the headland like an expert. I've described them often enough to her but she's never had to steer through them herself.

The bay is very quiet, the gulls louder than normal in the shush between each blast of wind. Greasy-knuckle rocks stick out of the hillsides, on a level with billows of dark clouds that curl at the edges and sit like a run of Atlantic rollers about to crash down over the bay. Yet the sun finds a gap and, as it spills down, Laggandall lights up like a pantomime stage, all the pink and blue and yellow-painted houses made too vivid by the hard beam of light. The town is all jolly and seasidey against the crawling black, as if it hasn't looked up and noticed there's a raging storm about to burst.

Meera is standing on The Curried Chip's tiny balcony as we row in. I know it's her because a tiny tornado of flame-red chiffon whips up against the white-washed wall.

And then, massed below her, I see the people – a dark, moving wave of them going right past The Curried Chip and the churches, glutting into a crowd at the harbour. It looks like the whole town is out, watching, as we drag ourselves up the Sound.

I remember Murray, dark-faced and angry in the hallway the other day, warning me about the subs that would rise up like whales from the sea, promising he'd smash up the boat, whatever it took, to stop me going out in the Sound. I imagine Mr Dow phoning home to say I'm truanting, Mum rushing off to Lena and Murray's in a state, not knowing where I am. She'd go to them first rather than the base to tell Dad.

'No,' I breathe. 'All that's not for us. Not the whole town. It must be something else.'

Ebbie and I lock glances and see a reflection in each other's eyes of that terrifying moment in the coorie cove when we wondered if we were at war. And once again I see the eyes of the dead seal.

'A trawler.' My voice breaks.

What we saw in the coorie cove wasn't a naval exercise, it was an air-sea rescue.

The mass of silent people that line the bay ignore us as we lodge the boat in its safe place under the rhodo-dendrons. Then I see Dad, hugging Lena, while Mum jiggles the twinkies in their buggy. I can't see if *The Magnet* is in harbour, but if it's a trawler it won't be Murray's. He's too clever, knows the sea too well, and he'll be wearing his heavenly blue pullover that covers him with angel luck.

But as I run across the sand, the stricken looks of my family tell me that the angels deserted Murray today.

Part Two.

The eggshell cracks

This morning, sheets of freezing mist lie across the sea. Murray is out there somewhere. The same thought drags Dad's eyes again and again to the kitchen window as the sound of each wave thuds against the glass. All his energy has fizzled to nothing and he sits, more still than I've ever seen him, listing seaward to the window, a faraway look in his eyes.

Today, all the battles between us are forgotten; today, the only thought we have is Murray.

If Mum was here she'd pull out the hoover and fill up this terrible silence with some ordinary noise, so I lug the machine out and Dad stares. The hoover feels like a sulky dog at my heels, its nozzle sniffing out crumbs and tiny sand drifts that have gathered along windowsills and corners in the night. Eventually I switch the thing off and it moans sadly into silence. I bundle it away into its cupboard and grab my jacket.

Dad rouses. 'Where are you going, Finn?'

'Just out,' I murmur.

'Your mum wants us back up at Lena's this morning. Maybe you can keep the twins occupied. We'll head off soon. Come and have some breakfast first. You haven't eaten anything.'

I sit back down. I need to know and yet I don't want to ask.

'Has nobody heard anything? Nothing at all?'

The only news has been silence. Silence from *The Magnet* since she slipped out of the radio waves yesterday. Silence as empty as the bay, with every fishing boat, every naval vessel and aircraft out searching the deeps of the Atlantic.

Mum stayed at Lena's last night while Dad and I came back here and watched the phone. At least, I did until I couldn't keep my eyes open any longer.

Dad clears his throat. The shadows on his face are so heavy he must have been phone-watching all night. He takes another sip of tea then speaks.

'*The Magnet* made a Mayday call just after four a.m. yesterday. Then all radio contact was lost.'

'Lost?' I whisper.

The Magnet couldn't just sink. Murray's too good a skipper. He knows the sea too well. Even at its most tricky, even in the racing, violent swirl that whips up when the wind is against the tide in the deeps way out past the coorie cove. And there was no storm yesterday, just roughed-up, soupy sea.

'There weren't any subs in the area?' I say quietly.

Dad stares at me and I know he must have had the same thought. And why such a delay between the Mayday call and the air-sea rescue yesterday morning? It was well after ten that morning. But Dad looks so wrecked I can't ask him any more.

I butter us some toast while Dad makes another pot of tea and we sit, munching and sipping, tasting none of it, unable to believe this is really happening.

People can surprise you in the unlikeliest ways.

This morning, Lena has amazed everyone.

She has made mountains of sandwiches and talks, talks, talks all the while as if there's to be a party just as soon as Murray gets back.

She's not the tiniest bit hysterical. Just solid-faced, though she jumps every time the door opens. Mum sounds sharp because she's trying not to break down.

A flowery-looking woman on TV is telling us how to make an Easter egg tree. There's one on either side of her: bits of twig decorated with ribbons and eggshells the colour of baby clothes. She tells us we must buy a carving ham for an easy Easter lunch.

Lena stops chattering for a moment to listen to the flowery woman.

'Carving ham,' she murmurs, and licks the damson-coloured lipstick she's put on. 'When is Easter?'

'Weeks away,' I say, looking at the fragments of Murray's last cigarette in an ashtray. I can't imagine weeks away, when we're all out of this nightmare.

My ears feel as if they are on stalks, I'm listening so hard for Murray's footsteps, for the oilskin crackle in the hall.

The twinkies, Danny and Davina, are getting under everyone's feet. It's not their fault; Lena and Murray's flat is small, cramped with furniture and toys, and there's no garden. I don't argue when Mum tells me to take them out for some fresh air.

The doorbell goes and everyone stills. Dad gets up and Mum turns off the TV but the muffled conversation in the hall is just out of earshot. The front door closes. Dad doesn't come back in.

Nobody says a thing. I think of Felix's insect jars. It's as if we're each trapped in our own glass prison.

It suddenly hits me that I should have known. I should have done something to stop this happening. I'd been given warning. What else could my noises be? What else did those dead jellyfish mean? And there was warning too in the dead seal, though it was too late by then to do anything about what I saw in those drowned mermaid eyes, staring out from a sealskin face.

I buggy the twins down to our house to play in the back garden. They spill out on to the grass as soon as I set them free. Wintry rain mixes with seaspray but the twinkies don't care. I watch them run wild, a hard pain all around my heart. They don't know a thing.

'Man,' they're yelling, echoing each other. 'Man, man!'

Little Davina is pointing up at the rhododendrons. There *is* something there. And it's not just a bird because birds don't speak in deep voices.

I lean over the garden gate and get a fright. The shore has sprouted a crop of bright-coloured toadstools. It takes a second or two till I see that it's really umbrellas, moving slowly across the sand. Then I see a man just along from me. He is peering into our garden through the leaves of the rhododendrons.

'Hi,' he shouts as he sees me. The rest of the umbrellas quickly gather around. 'Finn, isn't it? And these little fellows,' he leans over the garden gate, 'will these be your cousins, David and Danny?'

He smiles, a friendly smile, as if he knows us. I've never seen him before.

'Davin—' and then I shut myself up and stare back at him. What do you say to a strange man, backed by an army of umbrellas, poking about the bushes at the bottom of your garden? A stranger who seems to know who you are.

'That's my garden gate,' I finally snap, stupidly, as he opens his mouth again. 'Get off it or I'll call the police.'

That stops him. My sensible voice is telling me to calm down and just get the twinkies indoors. Leave the umbrella mob to peer through our litter-slapped rhododendrons if they want to. But Reckless is so fizzing angry he might do anything.

An enormous black camera pokes through the rhododendrons. The twinkies see it and immediately stop what they are doing to strike a pose and smile. I yell at them not to be so stupid and they stare at me, stricken. They usually get a round of applause for camera-posing.

I take the nearest thing to hand – a plastic bucket – and fling it straight at the camera, then grab a handful of stones from the path and chuck them through the rhododendrons. The umbrellas start to bob and toss as if a gale has hit.

'We just want to know what your uncle Murray meant to you and how you're all feeling,' shouts a female voice. Meant. Past tense. Suddenly I'm shaking.

'We're fine. Just great. Now get out of here.' I grab the twinkies by their anorak hoods and haul them indoors away from newspaper reporters and cameras.

From my bedroom window I watch the umbrellas scatter back along the bay like blown flowers on the sand.

'Fooshingas!' squeaks one of the twinkies, tugging at me. Danny and Davina are rainsodden and hungry.

'Okey dokey. Let's get fish-fingers.'

'One for me and me and me,' they are shouting, happy again. Who will tell them about Murray?

After fish-fingers I lie on the floor like Gulliver and let the little people stick elbows and feet in my face and stomach as they climb me like a mountain range. I'm being a raft in high seas, a trampoline, a punch-bag, when finally Mum comes in.

'Auntie Jo,' yell the twinkies. 'Look, Auntie Jo. We jumping.'

'Shoosh,' I hiss. 'This bouncy castle has just closed for lunch.'

I fling packets of raisins, stubby crayons and paper at them and follow Mum into the kitchen. She stands with her forehead against the windowpane.

'Mum?' I whisper.

'A submarine caught in *The Magnet*'s nets and pulled her down,' she says. 'The sub's sonar cable got entangled in the fishing nets.'

Pulled down by her fishing nets. The drowned seal in the fishing net. It's revenge.

'Four men drowned for one mermaid?' I slam my fist down on the table. 'That's too much. Far too much!'

'Finn?' says Mum weakly, and turns from the window. Her face and her voice put brakes on my racing mind.

I have to get a grip on myself. There are no mermaids. It's just a story that made the coorie cove seem an enchanted place, somewhere special outside the real world. What's happened to Murray is real; horrible and real.

I have to fasten my mind on what's real.

There would have been a moment, maybe even a minute or two as *The Magnet* was scraped across the surface of the sea, before she filled up and was dragged under, and in that moment Murray could have got out.

'They've got to keep searching. Tell them to search the coast.'

I almost shout the words to block out the whisperings and murmurings that are filling my head. They're too late now to warn me, so why have they come? Mum is all blurry-faced and concerned. I realize I'm gasping for air.

'There's no point, sweetie. Not now, not in this cold. And Murray couldn't swim, remember.'

He couldn't swim. Incredible, but he couldn't. He was as superstitious as Lena, as any fisherman. Learning to swim meant admitting something might happen to him out at sea. Tempting fate, he'd say.

Mum hugs me, and I wish I could tell her there's something terrible haunting me, and she'd shoo it away like she would when I was little and scary things seemed to haunt the dark. But there couldn't be a worse time than this.

Grannie Sand arrives and takes over, sitting Mum down, making impressed noises at the twinkies' crayon scribbles, putting on the kettle. As I watch her, my breathing calms and the noise in my head slinks away.

I go outside and sit on the back door stairs. The glittery granite of the steps holds a universe of tiny, fixed stars. I map out their familiar constellations just as I've done ever since I was the twinkies' size. A sharp, cut-glass feeling tells me this nightmare is real after all.

Grannie Sand stands in the kitchen doorway.

'Life can throw up anything, eh, Finn,' she says, her voice grainy as if the sea wind just cuffed her a mouthful of sand.

The tide drags up the bay and it's a sickening sound.

Top of the World

The peace camp doesn't have phones so I can't contact Ebbie. I'd have to walk all the way up to get her so I call Robin and ask if he can meet me at the harbour in ten minutes. He says yes, sure, he'll scoot down on his moped. His voice is as curt as my own. We don't say anything else and I hang up.

When we meet up Robin is silent and edgy. Usually, he's brimful of chat about the current girl or motorbike of his dreams, asking me for updates on the music scene. He's easy company, a charmer who seems to take everything in his stride, but underneath he's as vulnerable as me. The charm is a veneer he grew to cope with countless house and school shifts as his dad rose through the ranks of the navy.

But today is a day like no other, and even Robin can't act normal, though normality is what I crave just now.

We walk up the main street and are hit by the stench of hairspray on the wind. The door of Susie Snips' is wide open and instead of a row of wet or rollered heads the seats are empty. A hairdrier lies on the floor blowing hot air into a deserted shop.

Robin steps in and switches it off.

'Anne Marie works here. Craig was on *The Magnet*,' he says, slamming the door shut. That hairdrier might have been going all night. Robin looks utterly distraught, yet it's my tragedy more than his. I feel a flare of resentment as he walks on, wrapped up in himself.

The Curried Chip has its shutters down. There's nobody at all in the main street, apart from us. Laggandall is locked and bolted, hiding indoors as if a tidal wave is about to hit. The streets are so silent and empty, the desolation so huge, I feel it already has.

Without their bright umbrellas, the crowd of press reporters are as dull as a bunch of mushroom stalks. The pavement in front of the Laggandall Arms is cluttered with their bags and equipment.

'Flock of vultures,' says Robin. 'They didn't take long to descend.'

'I've already met them,' I say, kicking a camera bag as I pass and pretending it was an accident. I look up and Ebbie is right there in front of me.

'Hey,' she says.

'Hey,' I say.

A hot wave runs through me. I catch it and control it. I'm not going to dissolve out here in the middle of the street.

'Where are you off to?' Ebbie asks Robin, as if he's looking after me. He shrugs. She looks at me and I'm about to shrug too.

Then suddenly I know where we are headed, I know

what made my feet turn the corner into the street behind the Laggandall Arms.

'The Top of the World,' I say. 'That's where we're going. Follow me.'

Murray found the Top of the World when he was a boy. It lies way up in the hills behind the naval base, a flat ocean of grassland. When we reach it, the sense of Murray is so strong in this, his special place.

My finger taps his amendment to the MoD's NO HILL WALKING BEYOND THIS POINT signpost. Murray changed it to NOISY HILL WALKING BEYOND THIS POINT. He'd always tap the sign as we reached it. Right then, he'd order, do as you're told. The MoD demands it. So we'd clamber through the barbed wire fence, whooping and screeching, making as much noise as it was possible for a couple of crazy people to make.

I never could imagine Murray old and sensible. Sometimes Dad will pull himself out of a chair or Mum will be frowning over the account books, and there'll be a strange shift in my vision and I'll think, that's you when you're old. But I never once saw Murray like that. Never a glimpse. He wasn't meant to get old.

Ebbie is breathless from the climb. I turn her round and show her the view. We have climbed so high the town has sunk out of sight and the sea meets the land seamlessly in a never-ending, bumpy plain. And I see now, more than ever, why Murray loved this place. It feels completely removed from the human world, just like my coorie cove.

I look at it all as Murray must have seen it – distant and free from the ties of the sea, from the punishing bind of the fishing schedule. Yet with the wildness and freedom of a boundless ocean. Murray craved freedom the way I do but he never truly got it. The sea was a hard master, he always said. The hardest, as it turned out.

Up here, Murray would pretend he was on holiday. His holiday cupboard is a large fist of rock with a hidey-hole in its base. I reach in and pull out all his things. A football, a can of beer, a red plastic lighter and a foldaway stool. Once, in a game of football, Murray had booted the ball so hard his shoe flipped backwards in the air and plummeted somewhere in the sea of long grass. We never found it.

Robin opens the beer then looks at me edgily, guiltily.

'Help yourself,' I nod, but when he offers me some I can't take it.

'Where is he now?' I ask Ebbie. She hesitates.

'Mum says everything is on the way to becoming itself until it dies – then you just start becoming something else.'

'What else?'

Ebbie shakes her head and bites her lip. Then she hugs me, tight.

It's so unexpected I jump.

'Better start back now,' I stutter, noticing there's a silver cobweb lying on Ebbie's hair like fairy lace. She must have collected it from the birch trees on the hillside.

Robin is still wrapped in his own thoughts or pretending not to notice.

I feel a bit sick because that little hug has made me so explosively happy I could race about being the noisiest hillwalker the Top of the World has ever seen. And how can I feel like that the day after Murray died?

The murdering side

Jake is standing in the middle of the road when we clamber out of the rhododendrons behind the shops on the main road. I see him in the gap between Susie Snips and the library.

'What's he doing?' I whisper to Robin.

'Waiting for a bus, with any luck.'

Robin puts his hand over Ebbie's mouth as she laughs and we crash back into the bushes.

'Too late, he saw us,' I groan, but I'm wondering why Robin wants to avoid Jake. That's usually my problem.

Jake slopes towards us, with his shouldery walk. His shoulders move more than his legs.

'Well,' he says. 'You'd never believe it.'

I take this to be Jake's offhand way of saying he's sorry about Murray. I'm wrong.

'Does your poor widowed auntie know about the kinds of people you hang out with?' Jake asks me and nods towards Robin.

'Greetings to you too, Jake,' says Robin in an attempt at an easy voice, but I hear the tension.

'Pals with the murdering side, Finn? You're strange

67

stuff all right. Whose side are you on?' Jake shoves Robin in the chest. Hard. 'But then you're a strange lot, you Silverweeds. Your dad working for them too.' He shakes his head at me. 'Too strange.'

'What do you mean?' I snap at him.

Jake shoves Robin again. It's almost a punch.

Gently, I push Ebbie out of the way. Jake mutters something I don't catch and Robin crashes past him.

'What's your problem, Jake?' I yell in his face. 'This whole town's in shock and you're picking a stupid fight!' But he ignores me, grabs Robin and pins him against a shop window.

'A stupid fight, eh?' Jake stalls for a second. 'Are *you* stupid, Silverweed, or don't you know?'

'Know what?'

'You don't, do you?' Jake releases Robin and faces me. 'Ask Robin where his dad's sub was when *The Magnet* sank.'

My mind goes completely blank as I stare at Robin. When he says nothing and looks at the pavement I know it's true.

'Why didn't you tell me?' I blurt out at last.

'Thought you knew,' he says.

Jake nudges me. 'Let's settle this.'

Before I can stop him he's taken a punch at Robin.

'Jake!' roars a voice. Big Mack, a burly, sea-burned version of his son, advances and Jake slopes back to his suicide position in the middle of the road.

Some fishermen have come out of the Laggandall Arms. Each of the men shakes my hand as they pass by.

Their faces are full of emotion but they show no concern for Robin, acting as if they never saw Jake's punch.

'We've lost a whole boat family,' one of the skippers says to me. 'The boys are crying into their drinks in there.'

Robin wipes his bloodied lip and walks away. Someone puts a hand on my shoulder and when I turn Dad is right beside me. He looks straight at Big Mack and the fishermen, then nods towards Robin.

'The boy's done nothing. I want him left alone.' Dad angles in on Jake, whose head sinks into his shoulders, tortoise-like. 'Understand, Jake? Robin!' he calls. 'Wait. We'll walk you along.'

Robin hesitates, but he waits. Nobody speaks until we reach my house.

'I'm sorry, Mr Silverweed,' Robin murmurs. 'About your brother.'

There's a long pause. Dad is clearly struggling to find words.

'Thank you,' he says at last, and pats Robin on the shoulder.

Robin nods at the pavement. Dad nods at our garden hedge. Robin tries to speak to me but in the end he walks away without a word.

'Bye,' I call after him. I sound quite cheery.

When I turn back Dad has disappeared and Ebbie is in his place on the pavement. I'd forgotten all about Ebbie. She must have followed us down the road. Her face is strange.

'Things are going to get ugly. Very ugly,' she says.

'It's nothing to do with us,' I say, still in my oddly cheery tone.

'Of course it's to do with us. It's landed on all of us whether we like it or not. Robin, you, me. And Jake. We're all caught up in it, but we're on different sides.'

Her eyes freeze me; cold grey in a fierce, white face. Her freckles look dark against that whiteness, their patterns like star constellations.

'Rubbish.' I try to smile at her.

'You wouldn't say that if some natural disaster, a tidal wave or an earthquake or a meteor, had just hit. Well, this is a man-made disaster and the shock waves are only beginning. Nothing will ever be the same now. Nothing will ever be the same again.'

She gives me one last, blazing, frozen look.

'Bye,' I call after her, sounding stupidly cheery once again, yet I can hardly lift my arm to unlatch the garden gate. My limbs have turned draggy, sea-heavy. The weight of an ocean floods me. Once in my room, I keep away from the window because I don't want to see the ghost that stands on the pavement outside; the ghost of some old part of me that slumped out when Ebbie's words slammed like a rock on my heart.

Nothing will ever be the same now.

But it's too dramatic. Everybody's sick and shaken yet in a while it'll calm, then we'll all settle back into our ordinary lives. We have to. But what if she's right? What if this thing wrecks the town and makes great cracks in our lives that never mend? Ebbie and I might never be the same.

And that ghost on the pavement will stand there forever, on the spot where Ebbie and I stopped becoming whatever we were going to be before all this crashed upon us.

I slam any old disk in my Walkman, just to block out the sound of the ocean, because suddenly I hate the sea and everything in it. Starfish and sea urchins shatter as I rip and rip at my sea forest until the fishing net falls from the ceiling with a thump. I want rid of it. I want everything that belongs to the sea out of my room, now. So I hurl it all out of the window, tearing my hands on the hard bodies of the sea creatures, and close my mind to the picture of Murray that keeps filling my head: Murray on the ocean floor, struggling, trapped under the weight of his own net.

When we leave for church my heart is still thudding, my hands are torn and bleeding, and my head has dredged up Nick Cave's 'The Weeping Song' and is playing it in endlessly repeating loops.

And I feel empty, as if my soul has been torn from me and flung upon the ocean wind.

A town splinters

Ashok and Meera stand on the balcony of The Curried Chip. Meera wears a dark blue sari that's as shimmery as the ocean at midnight. On either side of them the crowd that has been massing in the harbour becomes a two-pronged fork that files into both churches. I watch people touch the Lucky Stone as they pass it on the harbour, and wonder which holds more sway over the might of the sea – God or the Lucky Stone.

'The whole town is out,' whispers Mum. Beside her Lena nods, her face glittery with tears in the light of all the candles people have brought.

The church is as cold as winter and very still even though it's crammed full. Sea thunders behind Father Marion's soft words and as he speaks I gaze up at the stained glass window with the fisherman in stormy seas caught between a mermaid and a god-like coastguard in oilskins. When everyone starts shuffling out I realize the whole thing has passed me by in a blank. But, strangely, I feel more at peace than I have in months.

Ebbie's is the first face that separates itself from the crowd outside that doesn't seem to know what to do with itself. Then a drum starts to beat a slow pulse and ends in a rushing sound that has the drow of the sea in it. Everyone turns to stare at the peace camp band who stand in a small, close group near the harbour. Felix is making the sea-rush sound with a long, wooden instrument that he turns over and over in his hands. It's a lovely sound, with a beat and run that soothes me like the sea used to. And maybe it's that, the sea-rush, that unnerves people because a ripple starts in the crowd.

A woman holding a black fluffy microphone approaches Ebbie's mum. Rachel shakes her head and noise swells among the crowd. Then I see the TV cameras, some focused on Rachel, some sweeping the crowd.

'This is not your battle,' someone mutters to Rachel.

'But it's theirs,' someone behind me shouts. It's Jake's dad, Big Mack, redder in the face than I've ever seen him. He's staring at a group of navy people. Robin is among them, with his mum and dad.

'I want to speak,' says a raw voice. 'I want to tell how my whole life has just shattered. And I'll tell you who's to blame for it.'

Anne Marie, her pretty face all snarled up, grabs the black blob of microphone. Big Mack puts a protective arm around her, his eyes full of tears.

'Every skipper knows the subs play cat and mouse among the boats,' someone else shouts.

'You can't take measures against a freak wave,' says another and with a jolt I realize it's Father Marion, speaking into the microphone. 'But you can against a sub. They shouldn't be anywhere near the boats.'

'Why did it take so long for the rescue? Six hours—'

A battle line draws up between a bunch of young navy guys and a crowd of Craig's friends. Skippers and navy officers try to get between them but it's too late. There's a crash of camera equipment and the television reporter's microphone becomes a stubby exclamation mark above the heaving crowd.

I'm yanked backwards by the elbows and recognize the woody scent of Dad's aftershave as I'm shoved over to Ashok, who herds me into The Curried Chip with Mum and Lena and Meera. He clatters down the metal door shutters once Dad is in.

'The twinkies,' I choke, then I remember we've left them with Grannie Sand.

But Ebbie is out there. I run through the back shop and upstairs into Meera and Ashok's small flat. In the dark hallway the noise of the crowd dims. I take the door that leads through the living-room to the tiny balcony and open the French windows. Noise breaks in like an Atlantic roller. The crowd is like bubbling tar on the road below and the media people stand on rocks, even cars, to record it. I lean over the balcony and see Anne Marie right below, her face rigid as she watches a skipper and a navy man push tit-for-tat like they're in a playground fight. I scan the crowd, unable to breathe until at last I see Ebbie, safe down on the shore rocks with Felix.

There's the torn sound of a car skidding and Constable Ross jumps out while the police car is still moving. He runs right into the peace camp's rainbow banner and keeps running, trying to fight his way out of the rainbow, as the crowd rages on.

Helpless, I stand on The Curried Chip's balcony and watch my town splinter into pieces.

Moment of contact

I jump out of bed with an energy rush that makes me feel I could swim to the coorie cove and back. I pull on my clothes, shivering as the coldness of the morning wraps itself around me, and wonder why everything is so strangely quiet. And then I realize why: the noise of the ocean has stopped. I tear open the curtains and everything is so ghostly it takes a moment to comprehend the stillness outside that's so solid I could be looking at a painting.

The bay has frozen over. The whole bay.

And now it feels wrong to be so buzzed-up and alive. It takes another moment until I remember exactly why, and the shock is so electric it's as if I'm finding out for the very first time.

Murray is dead.

Dead.

I say the word out loud to make it real and it plummets through me, a submarine weight with a sound as heavy and hollow as the drowned seal when we emptied it back into the ocean.

The bedroom door opens and Mum stares around at

my empty ocean walls and scattered sea creatures on the floor.

'So that's what the mess is out on the back lawn.' She waits to see if I speak. I don't. 'You need a good breakfast,' is all she says and smooths my sticky-up morning hair.

In the kitchen Mum hands me a pile of toast to butter.

'We'll keep to ourselves just now, Finn,' she says. 'Especially after all that trouble last night. There are too many strangers wandering about the town and your dad doesn't want our private business splashed all over the papers. So you can forget about school for the time being.'

'Suits me.'

'I thought it would.' Mum manages a slow smile. 'And Finn, I don't want anything else upsetting your dad. No nonsense, you understand?'

I nod and scrape butter on to toast.

'Those newspaper people have been knocking on the doors and windows all night. It's too much. Your dad hardly slept.'

'What do they want?' I ask.

Mum gulps tea. 'Who knows? I suppose it's just their job, looking for stories. It's a shame they have to look for them in other people's misery.' She frowns. 'You read things like this every day without thinking. Funny to think it's just a normal breakfast time for other people.'

'Now we're the news.' I smile grimly at her. 'We're famous. Two days ago we were an invisible wee fishing town, a nowhere place, and now we're history. It's like Lockerbie, Dunblane, Columbine – they're not towns any more, they're the names of tragedies and disasters. And now there's Laggandall.'

Silence falls like a bank of snow between us. Then Mum gets up and forces another smile.

'Cauliflower head. Go and brush your hair and find something to do that isn't trouble.'

Outside, the bay has fogged up into a blank screen. I cough, just to make the air move, to hear a human sound. I could be the only survivor of an ice age. Rocks glitter with frosted seaweed and under the mist and ice lies the ocean, as secret as guilt. The unearthly beauty of it hurts because Murray would have loved a strange day like this.

'Hi.'

I jump at the sound.

Ebbie is a throb of colour, stamping out cold and shivering under her rainbow-knit jumper. I have a sudden urge to grab her and put my face in the rough wool of the rainbow and howl like a twinkie. She stares at me as if she has X-ray eyes and can see the great bruise on my heart.

'Let's walk,' she says.

'Where to?'

'There's a film crew up at the harbour. We could go and watch.'

We walk along and hang about the far end of the harbour, away from the TV cameras. We hardly talk but it doesn't matter. Just being with Ebbie makes me feel better.

She laughs and nudges me to look at the camera crew. 'I don't believe it.'

Under a white glare of spotlights is Jake, doing his shouldery pose. He looks a bit unreal, as if he's a plastic version of himself.

'What's he up to?' I groan.

'Grabbing his five minutes of fame,' says Ebbie.

When Jake finally comes over he lights a cigarette and folds his face up in a frown but he's so trembly and red the attempt at cool celebrity is wasted.

'What did you say?' I can't help grinning at him.

'This and that.' He tries not to grin back. 'I was cool. I'll be on the news as a spokesperson for the young people of Laggandall.'

'Will you now?' says Ebbie but Jake is too carried away to register sarcasm.

'They wanted somebody who wasn't caught up on one side or the other to talk about how we're coping with the tragedy, so I never let on that Big Mack's my dad. They've already interviewed him for the fishermen's case against the navy, after that rammy outside the church last night.' Jake grins now. 'Too weird though, your own town on TV. It doesn't seem real, as if it's somewhere else.'

The outside broadcast is packing up so we head back down the bay because there's nothing else to do. Everywhere is curtained and closed.

Jake looks over the solid sea.

'Wonder how far you can walk out?' He steps on to the ice, gets confident and walks backwards.

'Fame's gone to his head. He thinks he can walk on

water now.' I'm laughing, yet remembering my even crazier exploit when I walked into a storm of Atlantic rollers.

Something screams, way out behind Jake, not a human scream. There's a whiplash crack and a white line zips like lightning across the ice. I recoil and Jake comes skidding off the ice at top speed.

'Imagine, they could have shown your interview as your obituary,' Ebbie smiles slyly, once he's safely on land.

Jake looks fractionally disappointed then slips into his hardman expression as he turns and sees Robin sitting on the shore steps that lead up to my back garden.

'Hey, Rob,' I call, and try a hardman expression of my own on Jake. 'I don't have a problem with Robin, Jake, so why do you?'

'Because it's like the end of the world in our house,' Jake suddenly yells. 'Our Anne Marie just sits about crying with my mum and my auntie while my dad thunders around, getting at me.'

I stop dead. I'd forgotten. So wrapped up in my own bit of tragedy, I'd forgotten that Anne Marie is Jake's cousin. How could I have forgotten that?

'It's still not Robin's fault,' says Ebbie firmly.

Robin walks over. His old, easy smile seems to have been permanently replaced by a tense, ready-for-a-fight expression. Still he doesn't meet my eyes. I want to tell him that none of this has anything to do with him yet I know that isn't true. It was his dad's sub.

'Not your fault, Rob,' I say weakly.

He gives a hard laugh, but he looks straight at me.

'Doesn't matter. I'll still pay for it.'

He looks as if he wishes he were anywhere else in the world except standing here, facing us. And yet he *is* here. A wave of emotion sweeps over me as I realize how incredibly brave it is of him to face us when he could just hide away at home; and how badly he must need to see us. Especially me.

I remember now how hard it was for Robin when he first came to Laggandall. Jake and his gang would pick on him because his dad was the enemy, as they saw it, in the war between the fishermen and the navy over the seas around the bay. But Rob would use his easy-going charm to avoid a fight and soon he was swapping motorbike magazines with Jake, until Jake forgot he ever picked on him. Robin never forgot though; like he never forgot I'd always stood beside him against Jake, in a quiet and totally useless kind of way.

'If it makes you happier, Jake, it's like the end of the world in our house too,' says Robin. 'They've taken my dad to the base for investigation. I don't know what's going to happen to him. And my mum's getting phone calls.' He hesitates, then stares at Jake. 'People threatening her, reporters hassling her. It's making her ill. And she's a good friend of Anne Marie's mum, remember. Or she was.'

Jake stares at his feet. Nods his head a fraction.

'You wouldn't know anything about my mum's phone calls, Jake?' says Robin, and there's a fighting edge in his voice.

'Not me,' says Jake, but he's sullen and uneasy. 'Not

me,' and as he looks at each of us in turn I believe him, though I would bet he knows something about it.

In Laggandall we're all linked up. The connections are as intricate as a spider's web. It feels like someone just threw a rock through that web and wrecked it.

There's a sudden clatter of hailstones and we run for shelter in the rhododendrons. Crammed together, we listen to them drum an ancient warbeat upon the frozen sea.

'It's just a fluke, isn't it?' says Robin, all of a sudden. 'People are saying tragedy falls in the wake of a comet. But it's odd, isn't it? I mean, what are the odds in all the history of the world of this happening here, now, with the comet hanging over us? What are the odds of catching a sub in your fishing nets? That sub, that boat?'

Ebbie puts her hand in his. 'It's chance,' she says. 'The supreme law of the universe is chance. Someone gets struck by lightning, someone wins the lottery – the chances are millions to one.'

'But the peace camp warned this could happen,' persists Robin. 'That's why you're all here. Maybe that's why the comet's here too. It was a warning and we ignored it, like we ignored you.'

As the noise of the hailstorm dies, a murmur starts in my head, like a taunt. Too late, far too late to warn me now. And then, as it builds, I get angry. Who do you think you are, invading me like this? If you're some kind of psychic warning, you weren't much use, were you? And if you're something else, some kind of psychotic sickness, I've had it with you too. I want my head back. I'm going to drive you out.

For some reason, Ebbie's psychotic cats start lining up in my head. A whole army of them. Black cats, white cats, Siamese cats, grinning cartoon cats, tigerish cats, sleek wildcats with fangs – all of them unpredictable, shimmering, psychotic cats, capable of anything. They gang up along an imaginary shoreline striking fierce cat poses and, amazingly, the noise in my head sinks back to its depths with a lame whisper.

I'm so gobsmacked I hiccup out something that's halfway between a sob and a laugh. The others stare.

'Let's do something,' cries Jake, looking freaked. He can cope with violence but not emotion. He panics, and crashes out of the rhododendrons, arms flapping like a stranded seagull as he looks for inspiration on the hail-crusted shore.

'Sticks! Bonfire!' he suddenly yells, and begins scuffing up a pile of driftwood with his feet. Robin hesitates then crouches to stack up Jake's mess into a bonfire. Jake kneels beside him to work on it with his lighter. It takes a while for the cold, damp wood to crackle to life but the heat grows, warming us, as the mist turns salmon and dark closes in.

'Do you know the word disaster means a malevolent astral influence?' says Ebbie. 'It's from the Italian for star: astro.'

'You looked it up? Ebbie, you looked up a dictionary in the middle of all this?' She's unbelievable.

Her head droops. 'I didn't know what else to do,' she says, and I feel a rat. It's just what Ebbie does.

'There are no stars,' says Robin. 'They've all gone.'

I search the sky. No comet either. Yes, it should be black tonight, the whole world black.

I smile at Ebbie but she still looks awkward.

'OK, what else have you been looking up? Do you know –' I start her off.

She pretends to take a huff then can't resist.

'Do you know we're all here because we've had exceptional ancestors? Not one of them was eaten by a wild cat, ate the wrong kind of berry or got killed in battle – at least not until they'd had children.'

We digest that.

I stare at the flames, remembering one of Grannie's stories.

'Do you know what a needfire is?'

The others look at me blankly.

'An ancient fire ritual for times of calamity,' I tell them. 'The needfire burns out the bad forces that made the thing happen.'

I expect them all to laugh but they don't.

'Let's do it,' says Robin.

'Yeah,' says Jake.

'What exactly do we do?' asks Ebbie.

I'm a bit taken aback as I didn't expect them all to go for it. I try to remember how it works.

'First, we have to look at the fire until our eyes burn. That's to cleanse the mind of the horror.'

We gaze into the flames until our eyes sting and water.

'Now we're supposed to leap the needfire to get rid of any evil forces that cling to us.'

'No problem,' says Jake, but he stalls. The fire is fairly

low now but there's still a good chance we'll turn ourselves into human comets.

'Basic physics,' says Ebbie. She takes a run before I can stop her, zips through the flames and does a rollover landing on the sand.

'You OK?' I gasp.

She grins. 'Impetus and momentum. The force of a moving body can defy the elements.'

Jake looks blank so I translate. 'Go fast.'

We all have to do it now. We'd rather risk burning to a frazzle than let a girl steal our thunder. One by one Robin, Jake and I zip through the fire and crashland on the sand.

'Easy,' I say, but my legs are trembling. 'Right, now we have to scatter the embers to drive the bad forces far from Laggandall.'

So we turn the needfire into flaming missiles. I take a burning stick and fling it on the frozen sea. There's a sizzling sound as fire and ice meet, a battling moment of contact when they are neither one thing nor another. And I find myself face to face with the thought of that moment of contact Murray must have known – that instant when his life met his death.

Furiously, I begin to kick the entire bonfire on to the ice and for one amazing moment the frozen sea is ablaze. The others stop to watch.

'No one else on earth saw that,' says Ebbie, once the ice-fire dies. 'Only us.'

Our eyes meet and a pulsebeat passes between us.

'Strange and beautiful,' says Robin.

Suddenly I've had enough of black thoughts and

misery. The needfire has burned them away. I want some action. And a good blast of music.

'There's something extremely strange in my boatshed, though I'm not sure how beautiful she is.'

'She?' Jake falls for it.

Robin chortles. He's seen my junk machine in its early stages but he'll get a shock when he sees her now.

'He spends hours with her, every night,' he tells Ebbie.

Ebbie knows I scavenge sea junk and make things from it but I've kept my increasingly odd creations of these last months to myself because, on top of my noise problem, she might give me up as a complete headcase. It's odd, I know, but it gives me a real buzz. The challenge is to see what I can make of the most unlikely assortment of junk – a lot more exciting than Robin endlessly taking his moped apart just to polish it and put it all back together again, or Ebbie looking for the secrets of the universe in a book, or Jake finding a hundred ways to catalogue his CD collection.

'She's junk, real trash.' Robin laughs at his own joke.

I make them stand outside the boatshed while I light the paraffin lamp.

'Oh-my-God,' says Ebbie. 'What is *that*?'

I can see my junk monster through her eyes because every time I've opened the shed door lately I've been shocked by the ridiculous proportions she's grown to. This is the greatest, wackiest, most amazing thing I've ever made.

'Stop the world,' drawls Jake.

'Stupendous,' gapes Robin.

'What is it – a time machine?' Ebbie demands, mystified.

I laugh. All the broken clocks do give her the look of a time machine. Then I see the thought zip across Ebbie's face before she can hide it. Finn really is mad.

Robin just grins. 'If you weren't a bit odd,' he once said, 'you'd just be one of Jake's gang and then we'd never have been friends.'

They walk around, probing bits of the junk machine and I flinch at every touch. I remember Lena when the twinkies were newborns, hating people fingering them and breathing over them.

'So what *is* it?' Ebbie stares into the birdcage body with its display of polished gull skulls, and shudders.

'Don't know,' I answer feebly. 'I really don't. But she's my best yet.'

Ebbie is looking at me in a way she didn't even after I threw my wobbly in The Curried Chip. 'Does it *do* anything?'

'Do anything?' I grin.

I release the pram wheel from its catch and it whirls. My awesome junk creature stirs into life.

'Finn!'

We all jump at Dad's voice behind us. I don't want to look at his face as he takes in the spectacle of my junk monster. Her great, moony face with its clock eyes and telephone-handle nose looms towards him and he steps back.

'Switch it off.'

I can't. Once she's off, she's off.

'I didn't realize this silly hobby of yours had got so . . .' Dad flounders, at a loss for words.

'Awesome?' suggests Jake.

'Ridiculous,' snaps Dad, but he looks as amazed as the others when the junk creature begins her bedlam of clock alarms and the gull skulls spin wildly on their umbrella spokes.

He turns to me. '*Switch it off.*'

'*I can't.*'

By some lucky streak of fate, something jams in the creature's mechanism and she freezes.

'Thank you,' Dad unintentionally addresses the machine.

A sound like a half-strangled gull squawk breaks the tension. Grannie Sand squeezes in behind Ebbie. She makes the odd noise again then breaks into a human laugh and puts an arm around me protectively, proudly. 'Finn, I never knew. Never knew you had such talent.'

'Talent –' Dad begins.

'Hush!' Grannie Sand is fierce. She tosses her cob-webby hair. 'Maybe not so much talent. Maybe Finn has a kind of genius – to make such a thing out of sea gifts, out of all the broken things the rest of the world threw away.'

'And what *is* it?' Dad demands. 'What do you call it apart from a useless carry-on that keeps him off his schoolwork?'

Grannie Sand pauses then her eyes light up.

'I call it a kickshaws,' she pronounces.

'A *what*?' everyone says.

'A kickshaws. You must know it. A kickshaws is a

peculiar something-or-other. It's from the French *"quelque chose"*.'

For the first time I look at my creation with a kind of awestruck pride. Usually, I sneak out to the boatshed feeling embarrassed by my passionate attachment to a junk machine. Now she has a name.

'Kickshaws.' I'm smiling at her like a proud father. 'So that's who you are.'

And then I see Dad glancing from Kickshaws to me with the strangest expression on his face; a fascinated, awestruck kind of look, like a father seeing his son for the very first time.

*Wizardry and
sea spells*

Days are shapeless since the adults shut their doors on
the world and all the normal routines slipped – even
school.

Mornings, me and Ebbie and Robin meet up on the
shore and scavenge for sea junk. When our stomachs
tell us it's lunchtime we go up to The Curried Chip,
where Meera is frying up for the crowd of reporters that
wander about annoying people. Meera will smile gently
to show she's forgiven me, after all that's happened, but
Ashok always goes into the back shop when he sees me.
I can't blame him.

Afternoons, we clean up the bits of junk we've scavenged, yet it's only once dark falls that the whole day
comes together as we gather round Kickshaws to work
some more on her amazing mechanism.

Yesterday we dismantled the boatshed plank by plank
because she'd outgrown it and now she sits, exposed and
majestic, out on the sands. She draws us all to her like
there's a hidden magnet in her mechanism. The harbour
gang come over to watch; they hand round crisps and
cans and cigarettes, and make driftwood bonfires that

keep our fingers from freezing. And we blast out music that shatters the dark – blue and blistering jazz stews that Murray lent me, guitar-buzzed oceans of sound, jangly pop, dark soul – everything. Music so good and loud it should crack that solid sea.

Some nights we make a massive bonfire that blazes up all Kickshaws' metal bits, or we stud the shore with a necklace of fire jewels. Then Grannie Sand will come along and weave her ancient tales into the quiet stretches of music.

We stay out as late as we like, burning away the bad forces with our needfires, making a kind of magic out of sea junk, while Laggandall lies dark and troubled behind us.

It feels like wizardry.

'Oh, get lost,' I mutter as the crowd of reporters, who have been hanging about at the harbour, look down the bay towards us. Those vultures just don't get it: no matter how hard they plead, no matter how much money they try to throw at us, none of us is talking.

'Needfires don't work after all,' says Ebbie. 'It didn't burn out those evil forces. Mum says they're stirring up all sorts of conspiracy theories, playing on the people's emotions.'

'The town won't talk,' I insist. 'They'd never let their men down.'

'Those reporters are going to be around for a while though. A public inquiry's been started and they're raising *The Magnet*,' Robin says, as we connect up an illuminated, spinning globe that will sit inside

Kickshaws' birdcage chest in the place of a heart. An illuminated, spinning earth heart – Ebbie's masterstroke.

I stare at Robin through the birdcage. 'Raising her? Why?'

I feel a bit sick. It's like digging up a fresh coffin.

Robin keeps his eyes on the globe he's trying to steady on its axis. 'The investigation needs the boat for examination. They've done all they can with underwater videos, and it's what the women want too – they want their men brought home.'

'What if they're not there?' I stop the horrible images forming in my mind before they've even begun.

'They've located them.' Robin can't go on.

'There's talk of a blockade,' Jake calls over from where he's lolling on the sand. 'If the MoD don't call off all sub operations the trawlers will cut off the Sound.'

'That's impossible.' I shake my head at him. 'I mean, how could they?'

'Line up and drop nets right across the Sound. The MoD'll never risk another sinking,' says Jake.

Robin clambers off Kickshaws. 'That's a brilliant idea.'

'My mum's brainwave,' smiles Ebbie.

'Really?' I smile back at her.

'Really?' mimics Jake.

There's an awkward pause before Ebbie decides not to rock things. 'Sort of a joint effort. An alliance between the camp and the fishing community means everyone's stronger.'

'That community will drop you when it suits them,'

mutters Robin. 'When it decides you're not one of them after all.'

Another awkward gap.

'Too right,' says Jake. 'Just as quickly as the peace camp picked us up in the middle of a tragedy 'cause it suited them.'

'It's always been our fight,' Ebbie bursts out. 'For years we've been saying the subs are a violation of these seas, a threat to your safety. Protect the Planet – it's what we're all about. If you lot had listened instead of treating us like a bunch of silly hippies, if you'd backed us up, then you might not be missing four fishermen right now.'

'Hey, hey,' I interrupt. 'What are we doing? This isn't our fight.'

'So you keep saying,' mutters Ebbie. 'Take your head out of the sand, Finn.'

'So you want us to start warring too?' I ask.

Robin stands up and kicks a bit of unidentifiable junk. It sinks without trace in a slushy patch of sea ice. He heads off down the bay without a word.

'When is all this to happen? They'll never get out in that.' I nod at the harbour where the trawlers are set in frozen sea.

'Soon as the ice breaks,' says Ebbie, ominously.

'Murray would want you to have them,' says Lena, softly.

She's given me a whole boxful of his favourite jazz CDs: Miles Davis, Chet Baker and so many others that are just names as yet but soon they'll be part of the soundtrack of my life. Tonight on the shore, once everyone else has gone, I'll play some to Ebbie.

Lena is at her kitchen table with a spread of newspapers. I peek over her shoulder and recognize the wedding photo of herself and Murray that sits on her television. There's another of Murray clutching the twinkies – a pink and a blue bundle – with a kind of desperate smile on his face. I took that photo the day they were born. I stare at it in shock.

'She was a nice woman,' says Lena. 'A kind face and really lovely clothes.'

'Who?'

'The newspaper woman.'

'You gave the newspaper those photos? You talked to a reporter, Lena?'

'I wanted it all done nicely. I wanted them to have the right photos and a nice story about Murray. It's happened, Finn.' She gives me a sad smile. 'The worst thing in the world has happened now so I won't have to worry about it ever again.'

I crash my boxful of jazz on the table, so angry I don't know what to say. How could she have sold Murray to the papers? I turn away so that Lena doesn't see my anger, and finger her collection of good luck trinkets on the mantelpiece – the wind knots and sea spells, rosary beads and prayer cards – all the superstitious and religious junk that was supposed to keep Murray safe. And then I see it's not Lena I should be angry with, Lena who has lost her husband and is so grief-stricken she probably doesn't know what she's doing. It's those heartless vultures.

The newspaper woman isn't here so I turn my anger on myself.

And suddenly I'm blurting out everything, sobbing, telling Lena I had strange warnings, that I should have known something was about to happen but I didn't understand the signs until it was too late. I tell her all about my noises and the jellyfish and the drowned seal in the fishing net: all the harbingers of doom that seemed to gather as the comet moved over Laggandall Bay. It's an explosion of grief and guilt but once it's done the relief is huge.

Lena doesn't say anything, just gets up and hugs me, tightly, as if she understands.

Harbour freak show

Deep into the night I'm kept awake by the gruesome sound of ice rupturing across the bay. Eventually I give up trying to sleep and look through the box of Murray's jazz music.

'A universal force for peace and understanding', reads one of the sleeve notes. Must tell Ebbie. I put it in my Walkman and it's just the thing for my frazzled mind, full of velvety, sax-kissed lullabies. It's midday before I waken, with the Walkman still on, and I'm fuzzy-headed when I make it out to the shore for my daily scavenge.

Kickshaws isn't there. Only our litter of bits and pieces remains – the junk pile, the tools and empty cans that outline the shape of the vanished machine.

My mind chunters, frantically trying to make sense of the empty space on the sand where she should be. I barely register the slow-moving procession of fishing boats in the Sound as I race back up the shore steps, along the garden path and then stand clueless, trying to think what to do. A junk machine can't just take herself off in the night.

In the attic room at the top of the house I fling open the skylight window and clamber out. Then I stand up, too focused and concentrated to worry about falling. From here, I can see the whole stretch of the bay and I'm very still and steady-headed as I scan every bit of it for my junk machine. Who would steal her? Who could move her? Though with her large pramwheels you might, with enough hands and effort, push her across the sand.

There's a crowd on the harbour, gathered around something that from this distance looks like a giant mollusc. Pinprick starbursts of camera flashes glitter round the lumpy object.

Slowly I sit down, gripping the roof slates to steady myself because I want to leap the distance and land on them all with the tearing fury of a beast. Instead, I clamber back through the skylight and race back down to the shore.

On the sand I find the wheel marks that I missed in my panic. With a heart full of fire and fury I follow them, running towards Kickshaws, towards the freak show they have made of her out there on the harbour with the whole of Laggandall watching.

On the harbour, I feel I've walked on to a film set. There are so many press and TV cameras. Dazed, I hang around the edge of the crowd that's ogling Kickshaws. I scan the faces, looking for Ebbie or Robin but it's Jake I find. He looks awkward when I catch his eye as he leans on his guitar case and flirts with an over-tanned blonde with a dictaphone who is old enough to be his mother.

'Hi,' he nods and slides away from the dictaphone. He's smiling, yet it's not the smile that you would give a friend. It's too edgy.

'What's happening, Jake?' My heart is pounding so furiously it's hard to speak. Kickshaws is mine. She was never meant to be a public spectacle.

'The blockade's on. The sea thawed last night and the whole fleet's out.' Jake flicks a hand towards the sea and I find a space in the crowd that lets me see the line of trawlers that stretch all across the bay. 'They've dropped nets so nothing can get in or out of the Sound. It's all-out war on the subs,' says Jake.

He gets increasingly twitchy as I keep my stare on him.

'I meant what's happening with Kickshaws. What's she doing here?'

'Is this your interesting friend, Jake?' asks the blonde woman. Jake's twitchy smile fades as hers stretches to include me.

'It was the others that did it,' he mutters at me. 'All the reporters were asking about your junk machine. It was just for a laugh.'

'Are you the ingenious young creator of this strange and wonderful object?' The blonde gestures towards Kickshaws. 'Kinetic sculpture, is it? Quite amazing. And I think you're quite amazing too, Finn. I've been hearing all sorts of interesting things about you.'

'Oh? Like what?' As soon as I open my mouth I know I should have kept it shut.

'Like you had some kind of premonition of the disaster. You had omens and warnings. Is that true?'

I stare at her so hard she blurs.

'Is this the one we're after?' a man calls. 'Finn Silver-weed? Let's hear your story then, Finn. Come and stand over here next to your, uh, machine.' The man nods to a nearby photographer.

Jake hoists the guitar under his arm and starts to walk away but I grab him. 'You've made her a freak show, and me too. You're poison, Jake.'

I feel as if I've swallowed poison. I feel sick. Doubly sick when I think of Mum and Dad's reaction to yet another public humiliation with every reporter in town ogling.

'Ease up, Finn,' says Jake.

'You'd say anything to get yourself a bit of spotlight, anything for a bit of cash. You got cash, didn't you, Jake?'

'Not me,' says Jake. He tries to shake me off. 'Beat it, Silverweed. Everyone knows you're a freak with your head noises and that machine-thing. It's common gossip.'

I wrench the guitar off him and feel the release of a pure white fury as it hits the water with the thud of a coffin. As the guitar plummets to the seabed Jake's temper breaks, and we're fighting. I hear cameras clicking, voices yelling at us but I can't stop.

I don't stop until Robin gets between me and Jake so that I have to wind up or I'll be fighting him. But Jake doesn't wind up. There's a punch, a blurred instant, then the thud of another solid weight hitting water.

Jake and I stare at each other through the space where Robin was. The rest of the world falls away as we watch the sea lap around the harbour as if nothing had ever disturbed it.

Robin doesn't surface.

Someone screams. Then Big Mack kicks off his boots and crashes into the water. In seconds, navy men and fishermen have formed a human net in the sea.

The reporters move in. I can't believe it – Robin could be drowning and they've lined up all along the harbour, shoving and jostling and cursing each other, hampering the chain of people that are throwing ropes and lifebelts into the water.

'I'm putting the harbour hose on that lot,' yells a fisherman, and he begins to yank the tap to full pelt.

Still Robin doesn't surface. I turn to Jake and he stares back at me with terrified eyes.

'I never meant it,' he gasps. For once he's telling the truth.

'Do something,' I tell myself. So I do the only thing I can think of. I run to the Lucky Stone and lay my hands on it and pray that Robin will be saved from the sea.

There's a shout and something is hauled up the wooden sea ladder, a sodden thing that could be a bundle of netting, anything. I stand on the Lucky Stone to see. Body after body splatters on to the harbour and then at last I see Robin, spitting water and peeling seaweed off his head.

The hose is kept full pelt on the reporters as Big Mack comes out of the crowd, soaked but smiling. He leans against Kickshaws for support and before I can do a thing there's a whirring, a great creak, and Kickshaws swivels her moony face round. The long telephone nose, alarm-clock eyes and seaweed hair loom over the harbour.

Someone laughs, a kind of appalled chortle, as the tattered umbrella we fixed above her head whacks open-shut, open-shut. The globe in her birdcage chest begins to spin like a world gone mad and the red bulb inside pulses a heartbeat. Her clock alarms start up their racket, and she is off.

All around me laughter breaks out in waves. I'm frozen in a kind of fascinated horror as Kickshaws unfolds all her bits and pieces like a great chrysalis revealing itself. Or like the twinkies warming up for a monster tantrum: you know what's coming yet there's nothing you can do to stop the embarrassing spectacle of it. And I can't walk away because more than anything I want to watch. I've never seen her entire performance.

So I watch as all her mismatched wheels spin and the polished gull skulls whirl faster and faster. The typewriter chatters nonsense and the suitcase opens slowly to reveal a headless doll on a bed of feathers, then snaps shut.

Something begins to bubble up in me. The bubbling becomes irresistible, uncontrollable, and I burst into laughter that's so hard it's almost crying as I watch the spectacle of my monstrous, ridiculous, stupendously wonderful junk machine.

Kickshaws grinds to a halt just as I think I might die laughing. But there's still the grand finale. The one we've been perfecting these last few nights.

The long, red wind beacon inflates as Kickshaws swivels her head to look out to sea. Laughter dies as everyone waits to see what will happen next, and I turn shuddery because the whole world feels as if it has folded itself into this moment, just for me.

The soothing sea runs of Miles Davis's 'All Blues' float out over the crowd. Heavenly blue angel music, Murray's favourite for a calm night once the nets were down. I picture him foot-tapping on deck while the others play cards below. He'd watch the fish flit like silver slippers through the great chambers of the ocean and swear Miles Davis brought them dancing right into his nets. 'Not a bad way to go,' he'd laugh.

I hope Murray went straight down, foot-tapping, on a calm night. Not such a bad way to go, he'd think; I'm almost sure he would.

The music carries out over the sea to the fishing boats that sit in spiky silhouettes against a slant of afternoon sun. In my mind I follow like a gull on the paths of the wind. The music travels the sea, moving with the currents, the notes tracking each other like a shoal of silver fish. I follow until the music finds Murray, lying still and peaceful on carpets of featherstar and sea moss, sheltered by tall forests of kelp. I watch the notes settle on him as gently as petals and somehow I feel at peace too, now I'm sure he's not lost and wandering in the dark of the ocean.

He always used to say he felt more himself at sea than he ever did on land. A fisherman out of water: it was one of his terrible jokes.

I look around at all the familiar faces, faces I've always known, and once again have a peculiar cut-glass feeling that I am waking out of a dream to find that this is who I am, this really is my life, a life like no other. One that's mine to own. But one that makes me feel like a fish out of water here in Laggandall.

The music ends and there is only the beat of the sea. It's a moment so powerful it almost dissolves me – the fiercest moment I've ever lived.

But it shatters when I turn and find I'm caught among strangers with cameras, notepads and microphones. They jostle, yelling questions about Kickshaws, about my strange warnings, about Murray. The only way to keep my life my own right now is to rip through them and run; but as I race home across the sand I realize that nobody in that crowd of familiar faces jumped in to save me. Laggandall just stood back and watched as the vultures attacked.

Scapegoat

Downstairs, the atmosphere is thunderous. Yet I'm sure to get hassled by the newspaper vultures if I venture outside. There's nothing to do except stick in my room, so I dive into the alien soundscape of Björk that Ebbie lent me, with the track 'Headphones' circled in pen. In between songs, Mum's voice rises from the living-room and eventually I go to the top of the stairs because I can't ignore it any longer.

'The woman took up Lena as if she was a friend, Kenny. Lena trusted her. She even brought the twins sweets.'

'Sweets? That's all right then,' Dad says. His voice is quiet but I hear him pace the room as if he's in a cage, trying to stop his anger breaking out. 'I don't mind so much that Lena sells her husband as a hero, but to sell her nephew as a laughing stock to the papers is a disgrace. I heard she got a lot more than sweets though, Joanne.'

I can't move. I don't believe what I'm hearing. Lena couldn't sell me to the papers. She never would.

'I don't like what she did any more than you, but she's

almost out of her mind with everything,' Mum cries. 'You have to remember that.'

'And a cheque from a newspaper will make it all better? What did she think she was doing to Finn?'

'She kept saying she didn't know how she would keep the house together, bring up the children. She had no money. And she believed whatever nonsense Finn told her. You know how superstitious she is.'

'She would have been looked after.' Dad's newspaper hits the floor with an electric crackle.

'Who would have looked after her?' demands Mum. 'This broken-down town?'

'We would have,' says Dad.

The room falls silent and the sea hammers on the shore, louder and louder. Once Dad starts his pacing again I force my legs to move and go downstairs.

'What is it?' I ask, though I don't really want to know.

Dad lifts his newspaper from the floor and hands it to me. There's a photo of Kickshaws beside an old school photo of me. LAGGANDALL'S YOUNG SEER is the headline. I chuck the newspaper back on the floor. If anything, I'm a hearer.

'I said daft things to Lena just after everything happened. I was upset. I don't believe she'd do this.'

'Don't bother about it, Finn. Everybody's upset,' says Mum. 'Nobody's in their right mind.'

'Premonitions, junk machines – I always thought I'd have a son I could be proud of,' says Dad, but the minute he's said it he looks as if he wished he hadn't. Whispers itch at the back of my head, and I panic because I just can't cope with a noise attack right here in the living-room. And then I remember that moment of certainty on the harbour. No entry, I tell the noises. This is my life. Go and bother someone else.

'I'm sorry I'm not what you wanted,' I tell Dad. All of a sudden I ache for Murray to be here, fighting in my corner.

Dad stops his restless pacing and stares at me. He lifts his hand as if he's about to ruffle my hair, but something stops him, some invisible barrier that we've built up between us.

'You're my son, Finn. I just want the best for you. Not this. I wish Murray was here,' he bursts out, his self-control suddenly breaking. 'Murray could always talk to you. You'd listen to him.'

It's just like that moment when I remembered Anne Marie and Jake were cousins. So wrapped up in my own loss, in my own mess, I've almost forgotten that Dad has lost his brother. And at this very moment his loss, like mine, feels like an open wound because Murray was the buffer that kept Dad and me from hurting each other, the go-between that kept us on an even keel. Murray understood us both.

The letterbox rattles loudly.

'Up to your room and I'll deal with those pests,' says Dad, as the doorbell begins a relentless ringing. 'If we say nothing at all, we'll get through this.'

'And back to normal,' Mum sighs.

Reporters are tapping on the living-room window now and I feel as trapped as a rabbit on one of Dad's killer fences.

'The back door!' gasps Mum, and I run to lock it.

The garden is empty. Beyond the rhododendrons the sea beats a steady pulse and I stay for a second to let it calm me. Before I can move a man with a large camera pops his head round the side of the house.

'Finn!' He greets me as if we're great buddies. 'You should tell your story, Finn, then people will understand. If you don't, Laggandall might never forgive you.'

'Forgive me? What are you on about?'

'You had warnings, Finn, but you kept quiet. People want to know why.' He gives me a smile full of fake sympathy. My head fills with the white noise of panic.

Come away, says the call, clear and steady and strong. I barge past the reporter and run to the ocean.

On the harbour, Kickshaws watches me row out into the Sound, her moony face still twisted seaward. Behind her, in the window above The Curried Chip, Meera is ironing. She lifts and lays the iron and it's such a homely movement it makes me long for an uneventful day in my old, ordinary life.

'Finn!' another voice shouts from the shore and I row harder. A figure in a rainbow-knit waves furiously but it's too late to go back now, even for Ebbie. If I go back my life will never be my own. Those reporters will turn it inside out and Laggandall will let them because I remember now that there is another ancient ritual for times of calamity.

The scapegoat. Some freakish person is picked on and driven out as a scapegoat, to bear the burden of all the ills that have befallen a community.

Laggandall wants to dump all its anger and pain and

guilt on a scapegoat, and since they can't reach the navy behind its killer fences then Finn the freak, with his junk machine and strange noises, will do.

Mist and seaspray thicken until the town is only a blur. I find a gap at the end of the blockade of trawlers and ease the boat through, steering furiously to avoid the rocks. The trawlers are quiet, the crews below deck asleep or passing time with card games.

There's a dim lamp of sun in a corner of the sky and, unnoticed, I row out towards it.

Mermaid kiss, siren calls

Seal voices haunt the air and dark is dissolving the cliffs when I pull into shore. Night has magicked the mermaid balconies to silver and filled the rockpools with phosphorescent glimmers. My coorie cove is more beautiful and enchanted than ever.

I potter about, exploring as if it's a strange, new place, wishing I'd something more appetising in my pocket than a bit of chipped Polo mint. Only when I jump down off a rock and crash into seawater instead of on to sand do I realize I'm in trouble. The night tide has come in and the shore has shrunk to a thin strip. I scan the cove and panic.

There's no boat. I left it on the sand, unanchored.

Surf coils and hisses round my feet. The sea is an infinity of foaming rollers, sinister and spectral, that boom into the coorie cove, invading every crevice, filling it with a savage force that I recognize as something ancient and timeless – the spirit of the sea.

There is only one way to go, and that's up to the black, echoing caves that terrify me. A wave drenches me to my knees, then another, and there's no more time to think. I scramble for finger and footholds but aeons of sea tides have made a honeycomb of the rockface and it's an easy climb.

No need to panic. I'll climb to the first ledge, then tackle the rest of the cliffs in daylight and make it home by land. Or maybe the morning tide will be kind and bring my boat back. Then again, the cliffs might prove impossible and I'll be marooned here forever, cast away in the coorie cove to spend the rest of my days as Finn the hermit. I'll live on fish and seaweed and scavenged gull eggs and end up as a pile of scattered bones in a cave.

Whatever happens, the caves are my only shelter from the biting Atlantic wind that's making an ice skin of my wet clothes. So I pull up on to the first balcony and force myself to step through the leathery, lumpen seals. In a black cave I sit and listen to their calls echoing through the labyrinth that tunnels into the cliff. And beyond the seals is a sound that freezes my heart – the sound of the sea murmuring and whispering, booming and crashing, deep in the labyrinth. The wind swirls the voice of the sea all around me until I feel I'm standing in a seashell and I don't know if the noises are inside or outside my head.

Come away, I tell myself, but I'm rooted to the spot, terrified, in the place of my noises, the place that sounds like the noises in my head.

Seal eyes glisten and I hear the slip of their bodies as they gather around me. If they *are* mermaids, they've got me now. They can do what they want with me.

But they do nothing. So I do the only thing I can think of to keep calm – I put on my Walkman. I press 'play' and my head fills with the music that Ebbie played to me in the coorie cove the day of the disaster. And in the earth-dark of the cave the huge, doom-eager songs break through the bars of my terror with their soul-rousing sound; oceanic songs full of life-wonder and spirit and fire that catch me up and speak to me in a music that is the language of my heart, the sound of my soul. Music that Ebbie knew I needed. Ebbie knows the sound of my soul.

There's a nudge at my ankle, and something flops on to my foot. It's a seal pup. Gently, I shake my foot but the little creature clings. Soft, velvet eyes gaze up at me.

'Lost your mum?' I stoop to pick the pup off my boot. It seems so babyish and trusting that all my fear of the seals dissolves. Mermaids are prickly as sea urchins and wild-tempered as the Atlantic, not gentle and lumbering like these creatures.

I step cautiously through the seals and they move apart easily, making a pathway for me out to the balconies. There's a sky full of starswarm and the ocean splinters into forever. It's like bursting into space after the black of the caves.

I switch off the music and the pulsebeat of energy that courses inside me tells me I'm not meant to be Finn the hermit, a mad castaway chased out of the world.

There's a call, a silent siren call that's as clear and strong as the shock of starlight. *Come away*, it says, and this time I know it's not the ocean calling, it's the shout of the world beyond Laggandall, tugging on an ebb tide. A world that is, for me, as wide open and unexplored as a far ocean or a galaxy of stars.

And now I'm all buzzed up, the way I feel when I've

found the final bit of junk for one of my creations and the mechanism's fixed up and ready to go. Except there's no way to set me in motion. There's as much chance of me rocketing into space as I've no boat and there's a wall of cliffs between me and the outside world.

Maybe there's no choice left. Maybe I'm stuck out here for good. If I was a seagull I wouldn't be stuck. I stroke the velvet body of the pup for comfort and it's all a-quiver. The same current is running through the other seals.

I scan the cliffs above and below and then I spot the thing that's frightened them. Too fast and forceful for any seal, it climbs the honeycombed rocks. Ocean light splashes on the dark sheen of hair that spills down the creature's back and I shudder as it climbs closer.

I never thought a mermaid could climb like that.

Sense tells me to hide in the caves but I'm held, enthralled and dizzied, by a stronger impulse. I want to see her. I'm just plain curious. I can't turn my back on the chance to meet a real, live mermaid face-to-face, even if it's the end of me.

The head appears on a level with my foot, as the creature hauls herself up on to the balcony ledge. I stand quite still – she's only steps away. The mermaid tosses her hair and there's a murmur of mer-music. She swings her leg onto the ledge.

Her leg.

A leg with a great clump of silver foot.

The mermaid draws herself up and moves across the space between us so swiftly I see myself caught up and smashed like an egg on the rocks even before I've looked in her face.

A footstep away from me she gasps and stops dead. I make myself look at her face. It's my one chance.

The fury of her wordless, wild-tempered yell ricochets through the caves, travels the winds of the tunnels, battering off every rockface, sending shock-waves through the rockpools and seals. I know that wild-tempered yell.

'Ebbie? What are you doing here? How did you get here?'

'How do you think, stupid?' It's Ebbie at her most spittingly, fizzlingly furious.

'But you don't know the currents,' I stutter. 'You could've smashed off the rocks at the headland.'

'I managed before. And you would care? I waited for you till it got dark, then I got so worried I had to do something in case you were out here throwing yourself off a cliff.'

She looks at me accusingly and I stare down at her silver boots.

'So you've decided to be Finn the hermit?'

'Decided not to be. Not my style.'

'Where's your boat then?'

'The tide took it. Where's yours?'

'Anchored, as you do if you've half a brain. Finn, I could chuck you off that cliff myself. You're so wrapped up in yourself, you storm off out here and never give anyone else a thought. You're not a freak show, you're just a one-day wonder in a couple of trashy tabloids. Forget them.'

I had forgotten. Once I'm out here the rest of the world fades away and I stop caring.

'I'm going to sort myself out, Ebbie.'

'Good.'

'I'm going to leave Laggandall.'

She is so still and quiet I don't know what to do.

'And where can you go,' she stamps a silver foot, 'with no qualifications, no money, no job?'

It's not the time to point out that your average eco-warrior in a peace camp doesn't usually have those things either.

'That's all out there. Look what you lot made of a lay-by beside a naval base – a whole eco-village. Ebbie, if I don't try to do my own thing then I've only one option – live a life I don't want and go totally psycho. There's nothing else here for me.'

Ebbie turns her back and I only just catch her whispered, 'Except me.' She shakes her head and all her hair bells murmur. Stay, they seem to say.

Something forlorn in the sound and in her silhouette against the glittering dark makes me reach out for her, overwhelmed by the strangest feeling, a feeling that must be Ebbie's too because it's so strong, as if two waves just met in my heart.

When I kiss her it's a mermaid kiss, all salt crackles and seawater. A tear-streamed kiss. A kiss that feels as endless as the starswarm and splintered ocean. It frays the edges of me, the very molecules of me, as if I'm one of those psychotic cats. I dissolve and scatter. I'm sea, sky, wind and rock – in her kiss I'm all of it, more than I've ever been in the whole of my life. And I want to jam the cogwheels of time, to keep forever in this moment where Ebbie and I have fused together in the peculiar some-thing-or-other of our lives.

But I pull back.

One small, wrenching step that splits my heart.

I pull away because the feeling is too much. I'm caught in a force so strong it leaves me trembling and helpless. I might disintegrate completely. Because I'm eggshell, too fragile to be in the current of something so powerful. It might grip me so hard I'd never be able to leave Laggan-dall. Yet Laggandall holds Ebbie.

I touch her face, with its galaxy of freckles.

'I need to sort myself out.'

'And you can only do that by leaving?'

I sigh. 'What will you do?'

'I'll survive without you, Finn Silverweed.'

'I might not survive without you. I might unravel at the edges.'

'You were doing that anyway. I thought that's why you were leaving.' She pauses. A long pause. 'I could come with you.'

Ebbie looks at me for a long moment and I hold my breath. But at last she shakes her head fiercely and takes my hand. 'It's not the answer. Everyone has to find their own path in the world; it's no good following someone else's. Maybe one day our paths will meet again. Maybe, if we just have faith, it'll all work out.'

'You don't believe in faith any more than you believe in mermaids, Ebbie.'

'Maybe I do now, because I have to.' She smiles and looks at the clusters of silvery seals.

'And you're sure your path is here?' I ask her.

She nods slowly. 'For now. I'm going to get my exams, then I'm doing an Open University course in eco-politics.'

'I didn't know there really was such a thing. I thought you just made up the jargon.'

'Well, there is and I'm going to be the best-educated eco-warrior on the planet. If I study from home I can help with the tunnelling.'

'Tunnelling?'

'We're tunnelling in. The MoD want us shifted but we're not moving. They've decided we're a destabilizing force in the community. So we are, that's the whole point. Anyway, we're going to tunnel under the caravans and dig a network of warrens in the hillside. We're going to chain everything together – chain the caravans to the trees and fix them to concrete drums deep in the ground. We're going to fasten our camp to the earth.'

I could plead with her, tell her I'm too messed up and scared to go out into the world alone; and then she might come. But she's gleaming with excitement at the thought of what she can do here. It would only be for me that she'd come, not for herself. It wouldn't be right.

'Stupendous,' I tell her. 'It's all-out war, then.'

'Eco-war,' she corrects me. 'Non-violent. Unless Mum loses her head.'

The seals call a long goodbye as we row out of the coorie cove. Deep below in the vast ballrooms of the sea the herring dance in shoals of silver slippers like they've got a secret source of Miles Davis. I watch them until we reach the troll rock.

Then I set myself against the Atlantic.

116

Adventurer and son

Laggandall sits black and silent beyond the red lights of the naval base. Ebbie gives a cry as we pull to shore.

'She must be frozen, out waiting all this time!'

What I took for a rock stands and wades out to drag us in.

'A full sky shoal tonight,' says Grannie Sand conversationally, as she takes me by the arm. Then she crushes me in a hug and I breathe in wafts of her warm, cobweb hair.

We walk along to her cottage and she settles me with a hot chocolate and packs Ebbie off to tell Mum and Dad I'm found. Once we're alone she sits across from me at the kitchen table and studies me like I'm an odd bit of junk she doesn't know what to do with.

'One day all these troubles will fade away and this broken-hearted town will mend itself. And so will you, Finn.'

'When?' I mutter, but already Grannie's hot chocolate is working its magic and I feel warmed almost to my soul.

'In its own time. Meanwhile, we just have to get on with life.'

'What if I can only get on with my life if I get out of here?'

'Where is your life if it's not here? What is it you want, Finn?'

'Don't know,' I admit. 'Yet.'

'Then you'd better find out. You know,' she leans forward, 'I think all of this was just the last straw. You were already reaching out beyond Laggandall. The coorie cove is the farthest place you could get without leaving.'

I struggle to explain to Grannie – and to myself. 'I feel caught. I don't want the same as everyone else here. I want something different. Something that's all me.'

Grannie nods. 'You're very alike. I've always thought so.'

Her words warm me even deeper than the hot chocolate. More than anyone else in the world, I want to be like Murray.

'That's where the problems lie,' she smiles. 'That's why you and your dad clash.'

'Because I'm like Murray?'

'Like Murray?' Grannie frowns and we stare at each other in confusion.

'Everyone in Laggandall has a love-hate relationship with the sea,' she says at last. 'That's the way it is. The sea provides and it takes away whenever, whatever it chooses. I lost my husband at sea.' She says it so matter-of-factly I don't quite grasp what she's said at first.

'I didn't know,' I murmur. I didn't know she'd ever been married.

'It was a long time ago. Your dad was only a boy.

Nothing sinister, just a plain, old tragedy like countless others down the generations. All forgotten now.'

'But your whole life is the sea. How can you stand to live here?'

'At first I wanted to leave. I hated it for a while – the sight and sand and smell of ocean; there's no escape. But in the end I felt closer to him here. I've come to accept that what happens, happens. Nothing is ever the same again; this kind of thing makes something different of your life – but what that something is lies with you.'

'Right now I want to leave because I don't think I can bear to stay. I want to find my own life. I made up my mind tonight.' I smile. 'I think I'm doom eager for the world, Grannie.'

'The egg of night,' says Grannie. 'That's when these things hatch. And what of your noises?'

'I think I've got the better of them. If I get away I'm sure I'd shake them off for good.'

The truth is I don't know what my noises are. Or were.

Some future echo, a sonic omen of disaster that chose me as its channel? Aural hallucinations I imagined up from the sound caves in the coorie cove? Or a kind of pressure-cooker release of all the unspoken, screaming tensions of being caught in a life I didn't want?

Maybe I'll never know. But I do know my whole life will be different because Murray died. Anyway, I've got that vigilante gang of psychotic cats at the ready.

'And Ebbie?' smiles Grannie. 'I didn't think you'd want to shake her off.'

'I don't,' I sigh. 'But she'll want to shake me off if I stay and turn into the town lunatic. Or freak show. Or seer or fortune-teller or whatever they're calling me.'

'True enough.' Grannie grins. 'An interesting career but not what we would want for you. But promise me one thing, Finn. If those noises of yours do stay around, you have to seek out people who can help you deal with them. You're not the first person in the world to have such disturbances. I told you Norse sea peoples tend towards it more than most. Promise me.'

'I promise.' I open the door and cold, salt air rushes in.

'You'll go to your mum's family? At least at first?' Grannie puts a rough hand on my cheek.

'Just till I get my city legs,' I tell her. 'Don't worry.'

'And Finn, you dumpling,' Grannie taps me on the head, 'it's your dad I meant you were so like. You don't see it but he's the adventurer. He did something different from everybody else around here, built up his business out of nothing. Murray was the wild one, as restless as a wave, but he ended up a slave to the sea like everyone else in Laggandall. It takes an adventurous soul to break with what's expected. Your dad's family didn't like him stepping out of line, but he went ahead and did what he wanted all the same.'

The door is gently closed before I can say anything, which is just as well because I'm speechless. As I walk the short stretch of sand to my own house I remember a conversation I once had with Murray on the Top of the World.

'Every time I go out to sea I'm on a brand new adventure,' he'd told me. 'Every day is like the first day of my life. Maybe today, I'll kid myself, I'll sail to the back of beyond and see what's there; though I know I'm on the same old mackerel chase.'

'That's what I want,' I'd burst out, grasping the picture he'd given me of a wide open life. 'To see what's at the back of beyond, not stuck behind a fence in a naval base.'

'Then tell your dad, Finn. How do you know he won't understand? You don't have to tear down his dream, you just have to show him your own.'

Tomorrow I'll be somewhere far beyond all this. And in what's left of tonight I have to try to make Mum and Dad see that breaking away only means I'm following the call that Dad, another adventurous soul, heard when he turned away from what was expected of him, and made his own life.

The fisherman sits at our kitchen table, bulky in his thick blue jumper and woollen hat. A shockwave hits me but the man turns and it's not Murray; of course it's not. It's Big Mack.

'Finn!' Mum grabs me in a fierce hug, puts her hands on my shoulders and shakes me, then hugs me again.

'The boy's safe, that's all that matters.' Big Mack cuffs me soft-handedly and winks. 'I was reminding your dad about some of the daft-headed things we all got up to in our day. Ask him about his motorbike antics on the pier – the night he'd had a couple of beers and ended up on the deck of a trawler. Mashed herring!'

Big Mack booms a giant's laugh that fills the house.

Dad rubs a hand over his mouth but there's no hiding the relief in his eyes now I'm back.

'But Finn, listen.'

Big Mack towers over me and I draw a breath of the sea-reek that's embedded in the knit of his jumper, ingrained in the pores of his skin so deeply you could never wash it out.

'Listen to your dad. Don't make the sea your life; you've seen what happens. You don't want to be a fisherman – it's a hard, dangerous job.'

'I don't want to be a fisherman,' I echo, bewildered.

'You don't . . .?' Dad crinkles his eyes and pulls his spectacles down from his forehead, scrutinizes me, then takes them off. He rubs his eyes and frowns over the spectacles as if they're giving him blurred vision.

'I've never said I wanted to be a fisherman.'

'I'll be off,' murmurs Big Mack. For an instant as he opens the door, the sea booms in.

I sit down at the far end of the kitchen table. Mum brings me a mug of tea and stirs in my milk and sugar as if I'm a baby. The spoon chinks on the side of the mug and the tiny sound rouses Dad.

'What else was I to think when I see you sneaking up the Sound day after day when you should be in school?' he asks wearily, all his fire and energy gone.

'What do you mean?' cries Mum.

Dad shifts in his chair. I'd always known Dad might catch sight of me in the Sound; I'd just blocked the thought with a blast of music.

'I didn't want you worrying about him,' Dad says.

'Murray was just the same at that age. The sea, the sea . . . my mother said the sea ran in his veins.'

'But Kenny, that Sound is a death-trap with those submarines. Why didn't you stop him?'

'He'd never listen. We both grew up through sea tragedies but it never put him off. He still wanted a life on the sea. I couldn't stop him.'

'Not Murray,' says Mum, ever so gently. 'Finn. Why didn't you stop Finn?'

'Finn.' Dad rubs his eyes again. 'Of course, Finn. But what was I to do? Build an electric fence at the bottom of the garden?'

Deep inside me something loosens, like a strange piece of inner mechanism slipping from its catch. And all sorts of odd, unconnected bits and pieces shift and reconnect, slotting into their proper places. It makes an ache, as if my stirred-up mechanism has caught on a nerve. The ache forms into a picture of Dad behind the fence at the naval base, watching me row up the Sound, his heart in his mouth. And he couldn't put his fear into words: the fear that I'd choose the sea as my life, and meet the same fate as Murray.

And now, just as he has lost his brother to the sea, I'm about to tell him I'm leaving. Yet if I stay, he'll really lose me; he'll lose the heart of me and all he'll have left is the empty skin of an illusion, a false dream.

'Crossed wires,' says Mum. She looks at each of us, gets up and closes the kitchen door behind her. The sound of the sea cradles the room as Dad and I are left alone to face each other across the table.

Dad leans forward a fraction and tension shimmers

between us. This is my chance but I can't find the words for what I must tell him. Grannie Sand is right, I'm Dad's son through and through, even down to the fact that I can't talk to the one person in the world who is just like me. We've never used words much, Dad and I.

Yet I must find the words.

I go out to the back steps to think and after a few moments Dad comes out behind me.

'It's a long time since we had one of our night-time sea walks,' he says.

'A long time,' I agree, and we walk down to the shore.

'Either you're out with your friends or busy with your junk models and I –' he pauses. 'I work too many late nights.'

The sea is far out now on an ebb-tide and we walk past the rocks to the sand flats that are ribbed with glimmering wave marks, like a ghost of the vanishing sea. I stop to look up at the glitter of constellations arcing above us.

'It'll be gone soon.' Dad nods towards the comet, much lower in the sky now. 'Maybe it *was* an omen. A harbinger of doom. Listen to me. I'll be getting Lena to read my palm next.'

'It's just a comet,' I tell him. 'That's all. Just a comet whose time came around. A once-in-4,000-years event whose time is now.'

And my time is now. I'm caught in the moment; it blazes in my veins. Once again I feel the tug of the outside world, hear its call in the wind. If I miss my moment, it might not come around again.

'There's a time for everything,' says Dad. I couldn't have given myself a better cue.

'This feels like my time,' I tell him, and with the calm pulse of the ocean to help me I find words at last – broken and stuttered – but words that tell him my dream.

When I finish, I notice at once there's something missing in the space between us.

'Walk in the light of your father, not in his shadow,' says Dad, quietly.

'What?' I ask, still looking for the missing thing in the dark.

'It's something your grandmother once said and I've never forgotten. It's what she told me when I turned my back on fishing: whatever you do just make sure you walk in the light of your father, not in his shadow. You feel you'd be walking in my shadow if you took on the business, right, Finn?'

I catch my breath. There's an odd feeling in the air, as if the ghosts of the past – Murray and my grandparents and all the lost fishermen – are gathered around us here in the dark, murmuring words over our shoulders to help us make things right.

'I'd rather be an adventurer and walk in your light,' I tell Dad, and suddenly I know what's missing. It's the charged, invisible fence we'd built up between us over the years. And in its place, fragile as a track of moon-beam, a bridge is forming.

Dad steps onto the bridge, looks at me long and steadily, really looks at me, then holds out his hand, palm upwards. I step on too and hold mine high, palm down.

'Deal!' we call, as we give each other the Viking hand-slap.

Then Dad puts his hand on my hair, ruffles it, and gives me the gentlest push forward.

Homecoming

Spring hatched in the egg of that long night. All along the roadsides up to the harbour the daffodils dance and my face keeps breaking into smiles because today the world has come to life and everything is on the move. There's a litter of luggage on the pavement of the Laggandall Arms which means the press vultures are moving on to some other drama. Out on the Sound the trawlers have broken up for now, to make way for *The Magnet*'s homecoming.

I'll be gone before they bring her in because I don't want to see *The Magnet* dragged home as a relic, to see Murray reduced to a name on a brass plaque on the harbour. I'd rather hold that crackshot laugh of his in my head or remember the boat-timber creak in his voice as he tells me one of his incredibly bad jokes.

He's still everywhere – in the noise of a trawler, in the reek of the fish crates. I'll be eighty-four years old, eating fish and chips for tea and I'll be thinking of Murray. When I look in the mirror he's there too, imprinted on the features of my own face.

So I can leave Laggandall Bay and I'll still carry Murray with me, wherever I go.

The whole of Laggandall is out on the harbour for the homecoming. The gentle sea-percussion of the peace camp band fills the air and there's a still expectancy in voices and faces that reminds me, cruelly, of the summer raft races in the harbour, when everyone waits for the starting horn. As the navy ship bringing *The Magnet*'s remains appears on the horizon, the crowd ripples into movement and people start to litter the harbour waters with flower offerings.

The sea is emerald and lit from within as if it holds a sun in its depths – a beautiful sea for a homecoming.

Robin's dad, in his commander's uniform, steps forward and presents Lena with an enormous bouquet of white lilies. She looks him in the eye for a long moment, then takes them and throws the flowers, one by one, into the sea.

Then the commander gives an envelope to Big Mack.

'For the families,' he says and offers his hand. 'Please take it.'

There's a terrible moment when it looks as if Big Mack will refuse the offering and the handshake, then he catches sight of the twinkies, fast asleep in their buggy.

'Man to man,' he tells the commander, 'I'll take it. But not from a navy man.'

The commander removes his cap.

'Man to man,' he says, then his face crumples and he's breaking down in tears, right here on the harbour, with the whole of Laggandall watching.

And when Big Mack grasps the commander's hand, with a grip that's almost brutal, his face is ravaged with grief too.

The bus sits grunting on the harbour and I fling on my bags before I say the last of my goodbyes.

'There's a present behind the living-room couch,' I tell Mum and Dad. It's a litter-crab, made from all the wire coat hangers, wheel spokes and TV aerials I've scavenged over the years, woven into a long, extending arm with pincer claws at the end. Just the thing for reaching sea litter on the rhododendrons.

'Come here,' says Dad. He takes me over to the Lucky Stone and places my hand on its ancient carvings. Then he gives me a thin, plastic-covered booklet. A building society account book with my name on it. I shake my head but he puts it in my pocket.

'A safety net. I'll be happier knowing you've got that.'

'It's not like you'll never see me again,' I tell him.

'He'll come and go like the tide,' says Mum. She looks wobbly but she keeps smiling. 'I know Finn.'

And she's right because there's something here in Laggandall that will draw me back like the moon-pull on the tide.

Ebbie.

When I walk over, Ebbie lets her hair scatter across her face and hides behind her curtain of braids. Robin is fidgeting awkwardly with Kickshaws so I grab him in a too-rough hug and throw a mock punch at Jake who is hanging behind him, just to break the tension. Then I pull Ebbie round behind Kickshaws. Her rockpool eyes are full and it's another mermaid kiss. I run my fingers through the braids to make all the bells jingle because I want to learn the sound and tuck it away in a pocket of my heart.

'Get on the bus then,' she says.

'Play this when he comes in.' I give Ebbie Miles Davis, Murray's heavenly blue music, and slip a CD in her pocket, something special for her to find later, once I'm gone.

The driver gives me a fed-up look as I stand uncertainly on the bus steps.

'Are you coming or going?' he asks.

I seem to be stuck in the moment, neither one thing nor another. I don't belong here any more yet I've no inkling of what kind of life I might make beyond Laggandall. I'm scared of the empty road that lies in front.

'What is it?' says Ebbie. She takes a step towards me and for a second I think she'll change her mind and come with me after all.

'Come away,' I want to plead, but I don't.

The beat of the sea is endless.

Kickshaws looks incredible, all her metal ablaze in the sun. If I can make such a thing out of bits and bobs of sea junk, then I can build my very own kickshaws of a life, a life that's like no other, out of whatever I find out there in the world. I know I can.

Then I see what's holding me back. Always, before I start a new creation I return all the junk gifts to the sea. It's a kind of bargain, part of the magic. And I don't want that ridiculous junk monster sitting here on the harbour, caught forever as a relic of a broken-down boy in a broken-hearted town.

I run over and start shoving at Kickshaws who is already seized up with rust.

'Finn?' Ebbie looks as mystified as the first time she set eyes on Kickshaws. Robin and Jake stare.

'It's where she belongs. Give me a hand.'

I take a breath and whisper a half-remembered chant from one of the old stories: 'Spirit of the sea, terrible and kind, take this offering and banish all the evils that have visited us. May they never come again.'

Ebbie flickers a smile at me through the birdcage.

It takes a good bit of shoving until we get Kickshaws to move her wheels.

'Now!' yells Robin, as she creaks into action, and we run her off the harbour.

There is a frightening crash and a great suction gap when Kickshaws hits the water. We're all drenched. It takes long moments for the sea to fold back and find its own beat. But now that wonderful old something-or-other is back where she came from. And something is leaving me with the gentle parting of an ebb-tide. I feel at peace, free from all my invasions and battles. The track of my life lies clear and open in front of me.

'Listen,' Ebbie laughs, her rockpool eyes full of glints and her freckles all sea-splashed.

At first I can't hear anything, then I catch it: a faraway musical burble as air rushes from all Kickshaws' bits and parts. The bubbles rise up through the water like melodious laughter in the underwater symphony that is Kickshaws' last surprise.

Ebbie's final mermaid kiss tingles and tears at me as the bus doors swish open and I step on and leave her: my anchor, my rescuer, my best scavenge ever.

For a moment, the whole of Laggandall turns from its sea vigil to wave me off; all the familiar faces that I've always known. And as I travel up through the hills and out of the cradle of the bay, I feel a rush in my blood that tells me this is who I am, this really is my very own life, a life like no other. I snap on The Waterboys' 'This Is The Sea', and though my heart is splintered, the music's great ocean of sound catches up my soul and gives it wings.

And my pulse is the beat of the music, the rhythm of the sea.